Yellar Boy and *Hey Finn*
Teen Boys in the Old West

- 1867 -

Tom Gnagey

© 2022

Family of Man Press

That
background stuff
it is always good to know.

The reader is about to join two teen boys along the southern border of what would become the Wyoming Territory in the mid-1860s, nearly thirty years before the area would be admitted to the union as the 45th state. Engineers had dubbed it's southern boarder the ideal terrain for a relatively straight stretch of the new transcontinental railroad. It was a region of high, green, rolling hills separated by lush, flat, valley floors. Surveyors had spent years laying out the exact path the railsit would follow. The always busy construction-head of the new track was inching across the area from western Iowa toward the spot in northern Utah where it would join a similar track being laid from California eastward. [See Maps on page Five].

Word had confirmed the earlier rumorreached the area tha tthat the *War Between the States* was over, but the bitterness between Yankees and Southerners would linger on for many decades. President Lincoln had been assassinated and the economy had been devastated by the tremendous cost of the war in money and lives and broken families.

Among the railroad workforce was a large contingent of men recently arrived by ships from China. They proved to be excellent workers – strong, tireless, honest, dependable, and – not typical of men in the west – clean of body, mouth, and clothing. They were willing to work for low wages. The lore was that one Chinaman, small as he was, could outwork two white men any day of the week. Those days were often sixteen hours long. Their pay was a quarter of that earned by the white men – just because they were yellow instead of white. Take it or leave it. In order to survive, most had to take it.

One of the two main characters waiting to meet you in

these pages is Kim Woo (*Yellar Boy*), a fifteen-year-old Chinese boy, suddenly alone in a frightening and unfamiliar World. He will fill you in on his story, presently. The second, Mack O'Henry (*Hey Finn*), a young Irishman, will 'fall into place' early on. Chinaman or Irishman, when it came to working on the new, Trans-continental, Railroad, they were overworked, undervalued, and treated like dirt.

* * *

Although some might prefer not to remember our country's history of painful intolerance and prejudice toward new commers to our shores – it has always been an ugly part of our fabric. Set in the northwestern United States in and about 1867, the story centers on these two, young, orphaned, teenage boys – one newly from China and the second, first generation Irish-American. Both were taunted and called hurtful names intended to put them down, keep them separate from the white folks, and to bring pain and humiliation to them, forever reminding them they were inferior in every way to 'real people'. Those were the terrible realities for these brave young men as they struggled to become productive and respected parts of life in the States. This is a story about how they coped.

MAPS of TRAIN ROUTE: Top shows the area with modern states. Bottom shows the area as it was while being constructed,.

CHAPTER ONE
Yellar Boy

As darkness changed the face of his world, Kim, contentcontent to be a loner, sat cross-legged poking at his small campfire some twenty-five-yards south of the newly laid track. He enjoyed watching the sparks take flight in the twilight, and burn themselves out leaving behind tiny, erratic, trailstreams of smoke – the only lingering proof they ever existed. The commanding, brilliant, light and scorching heat that ruledof the day, only reluctantly gave way to the uncertain, less reliable cool darkness of the night.

As the work train backed in slowly from the east, Kim stood to take it all in. It made at least one run each week, backing-up into the west for ease of offloading the supplies nearest the end of the new trackterminus. There were seldom more than six cars – mostly flat beds stacked high with rails, timbers (ties), kegs of spikes – and barrels of drinking water – always barrels of drinking water. The single passenger car brought workers and items they would need.

The working end of the line was less than a mile on to the left of his fire as the rails continued to push west from where it all began in Iowa. Once they met in northern Utah, they would form the first transcontinental railroad – Atlantic to Pacific – with arms and fingers to come, running north and south to draw together most of the western United States. President Johnson said it would help heal the economy, calm the chaos, and organize the riches of the treasure that was the West.

Well before it came into view that evening, Kim had heard

the lonely whistle calling out into the darkness and noted the clear, crisp, rhythmic clacking of the wheels against the shiny, new, iron rails. That announcement scattered the game – rabbit, deer, and such. Southern Wyoming was nothing but quiet at night. The train inched along, offering a stark silhouette against the never completely dark, blue-black, northern skyline. The steam engine was a wood burner, so it spewed great bursts of swirling white smoke high into the air. During his several months with the crew, the boy had grown comfortable ending his day with the billowingpowerful, white, cloud, the outlines of the gently swaying massive cars, and the rhythmic, clickity click, of the wheels.

In the usual case, with the fading of all that into the night, Kim was ready to spread his blanket and take his rest for the night. His habit was to arrange two small logs so they would burn through until dawn. It provided heat to the always cool overnights and kept the mosquitos at bay. He slept in his shoes – there were snakes – and he kept his knife at the ready beside his shoulder – there were coyotes and men with evil in their hearts. The Chinese men were known for their skill with knives. According to those who had watched him, that went double for Kim Woo who could stick a beetle on a limb from fiveten yards.

That night was *not* the 'usual case' of the 'usual train' passing on the 'usual track' beside Kim's 'usual spot' to bed down.

There was movement atop the passenger car as it passed – a man – no, two men – perhaps a man and a boy. They were struggling and fell together to the to roof where they rolled, first too close to the back edge and then too close to the edge nearest Kim. The struggle had gone on for some time when the boy rolled over the side and clung to the edge of the roof dangling there, terrified, like so much meat hanging in a butcher shop. The man stomped on his hands. He fell from the train onto the rocky, rail base. He screamed as he fell. He became silent once he landed. The man remaining on the roof, knelt and looked back as if to make sure what he hoped had happened, had happened. The boy didn't move.

After the train passed on west out of sight, Kim slipped his knife into its sheath, which hung from his belt under his long shirt. He picked up his lantern and turned the flame high. Expecting the worst, he ran with it to the spot beside the rails. A fifteen-foot fall onto rocks from a train moving twenty miles an hour through the night would not end well. There he lay – the other boy – unconscious and bleeding, his left leg bent awkwardly under him. He set the lantern aside and worked to gently straighten the leg. The boy groaned – a good sign, Kim figured. Dead boys didn't groan. He lay not a yard from the track, so, with a gesture of gentleness uncommon for a boy his age, Kim pulled him a safe distance away back onto the thick, tall, grass. Moving the lantern here and there close to his body to provide a better view, he found a gash and bruise on his right temple – likely caused by the fall – well, the *landing* not the *fall*. It was about the only mark visible at that time.

The boy remained unconscious. Kim examined hithe boy's leg – the ankle appeared to be broken. No bones had punctured the skin – about the only positive element in the entire development. He noticed the boy's hands, white as lilies without callouses – not those of a laborer. He seemed misplaced there at that spot that night.

Kim wondered if the man would leave the train and come back looking for him. ThatIt seemed likely, since it was seemed obvious he wanted to do the ultimate harm to the boyhim. The tussle atop the railroad car had not been a pillow fight. It had been the 'for keeps' variety. The more Kim considered the event, the more he believed that the man would need to know for sure how it had ended. He would be back.

That meant moving the boy into the thicket another ten yards south of the track. Kim prepared a well-concealed spot on a bed of tall grass with a blanket and water, then dragged the boy in a wide circle to minimize a telltale track in the grass. He was some larger and better developed than Kim but looked to be close to his age. He spoke as he tended to him, not sure how much he might hear and understand.

"Hey, my friend. My name is Kim. We are probably about the same age. You have been in an accident and broke an ankle. I can take care of that. YHou have also taken a bad blow to your head. You will probably have a pretty bad headache and may be confused for a while. You are in good hands. It seems there is a man out to get you, so I have hidden you. Remain quiet."

He gently cleaned the abrasion on the side of his head with water from his canteen. He bandaged it with strips torn from an old shirt. That done, his next job was to tend to his ankleleg. It wouldn't be Kim's first-time doctoring others. The white workers were a brawling bunch. After a day on the job they ate, they drank, they fought. Kim could not understand how knocking your friends senseless could be fun, but it never seemed to affect their friendships come dawn. Perhaps the blows dulled their senses and the drink made them forget. Perhaps their senses and memories were damaged to begin with.

Every morning there were bruised faces, broken teeth, lacerations, and several times a week, broken appendages. Some of the Chinese men called him, *Doc*. The white men, called him, Yellar Boy – "Come here Yellar Boy," "Take this to the foreman, Yellar Boy," "Mind to your kind, Yellar Boy. Stupid, Yellar Boy."

It appeared to be a clean break – the ends of the bones were not offset from each other even though the ankle had ballooned in size. Kim cut several, two-foot-long lengths of branches and pulled many yards of young, green, vines from the tree trunks, which he used like cord to bindsecure the sticks in place. The damaged boy was soon sporting one fine splint – one Kim could be proud of.

He did what he could to make the boy comfortable and returned to his own blanket by his fire. If he called out, Kim would hear.

A man dressed in black was squatting there in the darkness, rolling a cigarette. He wore a set of six guns and a black felt hat with a silver band – certainly not a worker from the railroad. His black moustache was drawn into smooth, sharp points, his skin was oily, and he had been in need of a bath for many days.

The sight of the man jumpstarted Kim's heart. Still, he offered his hand in greeting as if glad to see him. He hoped it all seemed genuine.

"I have jerky if you are hungry, Sir."

"Where you been, boy?"

"Nature called and I prefer to take care of such things in the weeds some distance from my campsite."

"I'm looking for a white boy about your age. He wandered off at the watering tower a mile or so back."

Nothing like a good lie upon which to build a new relationship.

"Sorry he got lost. A worker?"

"First time out. Young. I guess a few days on the job will tell whether he's a worker or not."

"Sorry I cannot help, Sir. If he shows up shall I give him a message. ? End of the work on the new line can't be more than a half mile on west. Maybe he headed over that way."

"Maybe. Just tell him he's expected to show up for work at daylight like all the others."

"Yes, Sir. I will tell him if he shows up. I may see you there myself. I've been working cleanup for a few weeks. Hope you find him."

The man spat and lit his smoke from the fire. He stood with some difficulty – Kim figured stomach andof side injuries from the way he placed his hands – and walked west along the rails. Kim was a terrible liar and hoped he had been convincing. Telling untruths was not a characteristic of the Chinese. They preferred to remain silent rather than doctor the facts. Kim was soon back on his blanket not knowing if he should lay facing the boy to remain alert to his needs or facing the track to protect him should trouble arise. He would not remember his choice, because he was soon asleep. Life on a rail crew was exhausting. It had been another long, hard, day among the smelly, profanity spewing, white men.

Dawn would soon reveal the nature of the world – dry but green, a full sun but still cool. He broke camp and secured his tightly rolled blankets and heavy pack to his back, before moving to see the boy. He wasn't sure what to do with him. He would give up a day of work if that seemed necessary. He wouldn't be missed – white men thought all Chinamen looked alike, suggesting they had never really paid attention.

As he grew near, he heard a weak a voice calling out.

"Hey, somebody, whoever helped me. Are you out there?"

Kim made it a point to raise his own voice in response.

"I am on my way. I am Chinese in case that might disturb you."

"I'm *not*, in case that might disturb *you.*"

As their eyes met, they each managed the hint of a smile – reacting to the bit of humor that had just passed between them – strangers of good will. What a fine way to begin things between them.

Kim dropped to his knees and slipped out of his gear.

"My name is Kim – Kim Woo. I have been working the rail-setting for a while. I do not need to know your name if that is a problem."

"You see the fight or just run onto me later?"

"Watched it happen, just that part after the two of you mounted the roof of the passenger car. I am not the nosey kind. I can live without knowing the details."

"You saw it all, then. I appreciate everything you seem to have done for me. Break or sprain?"

"I set it like it was a break – to be on the safe side."

"Thank you. I have a few dollars. It's yours, of course."

"I have a few dollars, myself, so I do not need *your* few dollars."

They exchanged quick smiles and shallow nods.

"First Chinese person I've ever met."

He reached forward awkwardly and offered his hand for a shake. Kim accepted it – also awkwardly.

"I hope I do my race proud in your eyes, then. I come from good people."

"I sort of got that idea, seeing all you've done for me. Anybody come looking for me?"

"Yes. I assume the man from the train – black hat, silver band, pointed moustache. He was clearly hurting – stomach and side."

"That's him. He's been picking on me for a time, now."

"Picking is something you do to your nose. That man was trying to kill you, friend."

"I got that idea, also. I'm glad I'm your friend – my name is a complicated matter. Recently, I've gone by Mark Henry – my attempt to leave my Irish heritage behind. How about you call me by my original moniker – Mack, Mackrk – Mark . . . O'Henry."

"Good to meet you Mack Mack O'Henryrk. . . . Henry. I imagine you are hungry."

"Sort of, I guess. Well, yes I am. I have food stuffed in my shirt. I'm sure you noticed. I can explain later."

Kim shrugged and pulled several strips of jerky from his own pocket offering it. He pointed to the canteen of water he had left the night before.

"Yes. Thanks. I have already wet my whistlehad some. You seem pretty good at fixing up broken bodies."

"Had some practice in my fifteen years."

"Me, too – the years not the practice. I have a thousand

questions."

"I am sure I have a thousand answers – time will tell if they fit your questions."

There were more smiles and chuckles. Mack unbuttoned his shirt and his food tumbled to the ground. He motioned to share.

"The break's at my anklebove my knee, I assume."

His head was still a bit scrambled.

"That's right. A clean break – *if it is a break*. Should mend relatively fast – *if it is a break*."

Mackrk raised up and slid back trying toworked to move into a sitting position against a tree.

"May I help. ? My grandfather used to say never offer a hand to help if the other person doesn't want it – doesn't approve it."

Macrk raised his arm for a pull as if to answer the question. They managed his back against a big, old, Hickory tree.

"It feels better this way. Thanks. I'll probably need a substantial stick for a crutch if I can trouble you some more."

"Of course. That was next on my list. Those saplings over there look to be good prospects."

He removed his ax from his belt and went to work on them.

"I don't mean to offend you, Kim, but like I said, I don't know any other Chinese, and your excellent English surprises me."

"No offense. I will even take your observation as a compliment. I spent four years in an English missionary school back home in China. I catch on to things easy – that is – easy – er, eas*ily*. Mr. Thompson, my teacher, would have been proud of me for catching that adjective/adverb thing. He was a good man – too religious, but I never held that against him. He meant well. Grandfather always said to keep your religion to yourself unless somebody asked about it."

"I suppose I agree. I'm not really a religious person. My brothers and I used to joke that our mother had plenty for all of us."

Kim shrugged not really understanding but thinking he didn't need to. More shared smiles. Though neither spoke it, they each had the feeling there was a good chance they were going to become good friends.

"Do you need to get to work? I can take care of myself."

"I have decided to take the day off so we can figure how we

are going to get on with things."

"Thank you. When you have time, Kim, I'd like to hear about your life – nothing you don't feel like sharing, of course. You interest me and, like I said, I know nothing about the Chinese people."

"No time like the present, I guess. Let me divide up some of this food. I also have bread, apples, salt pork in my backpack – not much, but it keeps a guy going."

"I can't take your food from you."

"A Chinaman would be offended if you turned down his offer of hospitality. A long-standing, centuries old custom. Some of my ancestors weighed four hundred pounds. Please do not make me summon them."

Smiles!

"A long-standing custom of how long, five minutes?"

"Actually, ILong-standing for as long as I've been me, at least. Our Chinese traditions are important to us."

"I like you, Kim Woo. Have I thanked you for your several kindnesses?"

"Both in words and friendship. It is time to put that behind us. Eat. When you feel ready, we will move to a safer and more protected place up in the hills to the south. While I make something useful out of this stick, I will regale you with the wonderful life of Kim Woo, only son of Ling Woo, my mother."

Mack noted he had not credited a father in his life. He assumed that in China it took one to help make a new person just like it did there in America. He would not ask but had to admit he was interested – in the boy's family, not how babies were made.

"I'll listen as I watch you work that axe and knife. I just imagine I will learn something useful from both."

""Well, I was born at an early age of mixed parentage – one male and one female."

Mack chuckled.

"My father was a seaman and left mother and me was killed before I was born, duringin what is often called the Opium War – China vs the British. From my appearance, I must assume he was English – white, at least. That makes me what they call a half-breed here in the West. Mother seldom spokeeaks of him or their relationship.

"I come from southeastern China, just inland from the South China Sea. When the breeze blows in off the water, the air is filled with a wonderful sweetness. I suppose it is my favorite aroma – next to mother, that is. She and I had a three-room hut with a good roof, a glass window in each room, and a fine fireplace – features few of the nearby huts had. Mother supported us by weaving hats from young reeds. I gathered them and helped by splitting them in half lengthwise – more difficult than it might sound.. Everybody said she was the finest weaver in the village. When buyers came from the city to make purchases for their stores, Mother's hats were always bought first. I was proud to be the son of such a highly respected woman. We made a very good life in a place and time where that was not easy.

"I had lots of playmates who lived nearby. When I was eleven, a small group of Missionaries from England established a church and school in our village. After the teacher talked with the children, he invited twenty of us to join his school. We did not have to become Christians, but we had to attend Sunday services. I found his stories interesting.

"Those next four years wereat was probably the most important four years of my life – my school years. He said I learned fast, and by fourth year I was helping teach the youngest children. I liked history and ILanguages the best, but I did well in all my subjects. I speak French and English in addition to my native Mandarin and Cantonese.

"During fourth year, my best friend met with a terrible accident. Our mothers had warned us to keep way back from the ocean that day – the beach was no more than a hundred yards half mile east of the village. The clouds were unusual, and the air was heavy and foul smelling. The view out into the ocean was blocked by a dark, low-lying, churning mist – something I had never seen before, so I became fascinated with it. Some change in the weather was certainly coming.

"We minded like most thirteen-year-olds and went directly to the broad, sandy beach."

"The waves are huge, Kim. I've never seen them like this.," Ming said.

"I know, Ming. We should run into them asdd the water flows out and see how far ashore they wash us as they return."

"I don't think so, Kim. Look on out to sea – those crests must be ten feet tall. Grandfather says such waves always come with strong, riptides. Get sucked under by one of them and you'll never get free."

"I suppose you are right. I have not heard anything about a typhoon, have you?"

"No, but this time of year, you never know."

Of course, we did know, but I would not argue the point with him. I moved close to the water – just enough so the edge of the rolling water rippled up and around my bare feet before it rushed away again. It was considerably colder than usual. That usually meant the colder water was churning up from the ocean floor. Everything about that morning was fascinating – strange but fascinating. We were too dumb to be scared.

At one point, a huge wave was upon us – a fifteen-footer one that burst through the mist and buried us both even though he had stayed well back from where I stood. It ran water a hundred yards up onto the beach where our village sat.

I used the rule for handling a riptide – move to the top of the water and flatten out on your back until the pull lessons – then turn over and swim across the current – never with it or against it. I do not know if Ming did not know the rule, or if he was too soon overpowered. I never saw him again. It was the saddest moment in my life up to then. I ran toward home fighting the torrent of heavy rain that had set in with the huge wave. Each drop stung my skin like a hot coal from a fire.

The land naturally became much higher some fifty yards up a rise behind the beach. I was well west of my house and realized it was best for me to hurry on up to that highland before working on a plan to connect with my mother. I hunkered down under a growth of bushes with strong stems and wide leaves. It provided pretty good protection from both the wind and rain.

Hours passed before the wind blew itself out and gradually the water receded, though it had dug large trencheholes which would continue to hold it and mosquitos for days. Avoiding them, I carefully picked my way back down the gentle slope in the direction of my hut. I could not even hope for the best because I was surrounded by the worst – huts and sheds just gone, washed out to sea. The village was nothing more than a plain of mud riddled with sticks and boards and pieces of clothing. And so, I *found it to be for my home – gone with the water.*

I ran here and there calling out for my mother. I lifted boards and shingles, and metal sheets from roofs. At some point I had begun crying. I found myself surrounded by a seas of what had been mother's beautiful reed hats. I reached out trying to save them. They were soon gone with the houses and the carts and the chairs and tables and cabinets. I felt no loss regarding such things, but my mother – how would I ever go on without the most important part of my life?

CHAPTER TWO
The World Took on a Different Scent

I heard a man's voice calling out from behind me.

'Kim Woo! Kim Woo!'

I turned and looked. It was Mr. Ling – he and his wife lived next door to us and were expecting their first baby. He was also crying. We ran to each other and held a silent embrace for some time. We knew what had happened. We didn't want to speak of it. Acknowledging death drains away all hope, and neither of us wanted that.

I managed the first words between us; "I think Ming was taken, too. That was mostly my fault. I encouraged him to go too close to the water. How will I ever be able to tell his mother?"

As it turned out, I would never have to tell her. Their hut had also been washed away with his mother and little sister inside.

My mother would have said, 'Ming knew you were not an authority on storms. He did what he did because he decided to.' It was true. It didn't help. It seemed I was determined to blame myself.

Mr. Ming walked with me to the stone and mortar school building, which remained undamaged. It was becoming the gathering place for those of us who survived – sadly a small number. The teacher headed toward me as soon as I entered the building. I did not want to hear any of his religious mumbo-jumbo. I should have given him credit for knowing me better than that.

"Kim. Gather the younger children together and do what you can to console them. They love you and trust you."

Looking back, I can see how wise he had been. He forced me to broaden my selfish sadness to include the needs of the children and let me do what I could to help them. I started singing a favorite children's song. They soon joined in. A girl my age added motions and marching and clapping and soon they were fully engaged in the distraction.

Several months passed. The missionaries arranged shelter and food and organized clean-up parties. Rebuilding had started. I had not seen Mr. Ling for a number of weeks. I hoped he hadn't moved on without talking with me about his plans. He was the closest thing to family I had left.

Before dawn on the Monday morning of the tenth week, somebody awakened me by shaking my shoulder. It was Mr. Ling kneeling there where I slept inside the school building. I was delighted to see him. He whispered, so he would not awaken any others. We were soon outside – I was carrying my shoes.

"Kim. A dozen of us men have arranged passage to the Americas. I do not know all the details. There is work there and a chance to begin again. Things are only going to get worse here. I want you to come with us. The Captain made it clear that no children will be allowed, but I think we can manage to get a boy your age onboard – crossing the first mate's palm with a few pieces of gold should handle that. Work and a new life, Kim! There is no future for us – for you – here. Please come with me. We just heard that we sail with the tide at noon today. The wharf is just west of the lighthouse jetty. It will be the only tall ship in port. Three masts and twelve sails, I am told. A good, strong, ship."

I thought for only a moment and agreed to be there. Even as a brand new fourteen-year-old on tiptoes, I knew I could not pass for an adult among the white crew. I had to trust Mr. Ling. Surely, once on board and out to sea the captain would not set me adrift. I was a good worker. I would show him how helpful I could be. What he might decide to do with me once we arrived in America would be a situation to consider after I arrived.

"My papers and a few, small, possessions are in a hiding place. I will get them. I will be there, Mr. Ling. You watch for me."

Mr. Ling left, clearly happy about my decision. I hoped I was. I slipped into my shoes – they were about my most valuable possession at that moment – and made my way to the bell tower of the church. It hovered above everything there in what had been our little town. It was a tall shaft that rose thirty feet into the air. At ground level, it housed the entrance to the building with two windows and double doors. The top was capped with the louvered belltower. The bell had come with the missionaries all the way from England. It came with an interesting story, but that is not relevant to this telling.

I climbed up from cross-beam to cross-beam inside the tower. It took some time. The wood was roughhewn on the inside and left splinters in my hands. I did not stop to rest until I reached the very top. My box had survived the typhoon. It was bound to one of the beams. It was wooden with a slide top – six inches long, four inches wide and less than two inches deep. I experienced a deep sense of relief when I held it in my hands. I checked the contents: my birth papers and others in an oiled envelope, my status papers (a verified resident of my village), a neckless mother had given me that had been in her family for more than a century, and a small, cloth pouch that contained coins I had accumulated during the previous several years.

I tied the ribbon back around the envelope and returned it to the box. I stuffed the box under my rope belt at my waist hiding it inside my baggy trousers and under my long shirt. The tripdescent back down to the ground went much faster. My heart was pounding – more from excitement than exertion. I sat and gave myself several minutes for my heart to slow and my chest to calm down, realizing I was about to leave behind everything I had ever known. Rested, I proceeded toward the jetty. It was close by, so I had no reason to hurry. There were very few boats along the shore – a few were moving passengers, some with supplies and others just taking care of business, I figured. The view across the water to the horizon brought mixed feelings. There was the familiar, beautiful, view – green water that grew lighter and lighter until it finally touched the deep blue sky miles out to sea. In many ways it represented the essence of my wonderful childhood – one side of my world. Still active in my mind were the horrible images from the day of the storm. I wondered if they would ever go away.

I lived with them in my dreams. I lived with them right there and then as they invaded and drove away the reassuring possibilities of the moment.

I arrived hours early and found a perch from where I could survey the area around the jetty and study the huge ship. I had saved a biscuit from supper and used it to quiet my growling belly. I assumed there would be plenty of food onboard the ship. I wondered how I was to find out from Mr. Ling about boarding – when, where, how? I had positioned myself so I could be easily seen by anybody who was searching for me. I maintained a lookout for him. That was my whole source of hope right then. My heart sunk – I was fully dependent on others who might or might not see fit to take care of me. For the first time in my life, I felt helpless.

At that moment, I realized all I had in my life were the box, the clothes I was wearing, a few coins, and a string of feeble possibilities. I couldn't reach out and touch possibilities. I couldn't hold them close when I was scared. I couldn't depend on them to take care of me. What I had were maybes and possibilities – maybe a journey to a new country I wasn't even sure really existed that lay far across an ocean – an ocean that was deep and dark and ravaged by terrible storms and the worse sort of uncertainty. There were stories about gigantic sea monsters that plucked boys out of ships and ate them for breakfast. What I needed was not maybes and possibilities. What I needed were a mother and father to draw me close to them and tell me things would be okay.

I had never been on a vessel larger than a sampan. I allowed a few fantasies around the idea that it – The Saint George – might have been the very ship my father had sailed on from England. Any thought about him became the source of an uncomfortable set of feelings – joyful, frightening, confusing – maybe pride. All in all, they were less pleasant than pleasant, filled with more uncertainty than certainty, and memories that were as much my childish fantasies as truths and facts. I wouldn't know where to begin sorting them out.

Two men in their early fifties wearing impressive, if gaudy, uniforms met and stopped just within ear shot of where I sat atop a section of a long-abandoned wharf. They offered right hands for shakes and left hands to each other's shoulders. It was clearly a warm greeting between friends.

""Captain Higgins. Good to see you again. I hear you're commanding the St. George. A good ship.".."

""That's right. What are you about?"?"

""I am waiting for The Duke of Tames to arrive with supplies for these unfortunate people. I will take her back to England with

rice and tea and opium. Few Chinese passengers due to the storm. Most don't have the passage. It will winnow out the lower class that tends to be rowdy and dirty. Those few who will be sailing will be a more proper class of men – the kind the railroad and gold mines of the American west prefer.".”

""Did you hear about Admiral Windsor?"?”

"Yes. Unfortunate fall, the way I heard it. May be laid up for most of a year. He's too old to be showing off climbing the rigging.”

""You have a complete crew, Higgins?"?”

""Not really. What I have for sure is seasoned. Many have sailed with me before. I'm told my first mate is on his way, which leaves me down a dozen seamen and without a cabin boy. I suppose I will survive without one.".”

"What's your cargo?" ?”

""The usual out of China plus a dozen or so Chinamen heading for America. We'll probably drop them off in Southern CaliforniaMexico. I like having Chinamen aboard – never a rowdy one among them. I sail at noon. Better be on my way. Have a safe journey.".”

""Same to you. God speed.”

While they had been speaking, a plan took shape in my head – I suppose that is the usual place for a plan to take shape.

Mackrk chuckled and changed the position of his leg. The Chinese kid had an odd sense of humor. Mack liked that. Kim continued.

I figured if my plan failed, I would be no worse off than I already was. I ran to catch up with the Captain.

"Captain, Sir. Would you be Captain Higgins?"?”

""Yes. I am Captain Higgins. May I help you?"?”

He paused his walk and offered a nice smile, which provided a degree of confidence to proceed to my next step.

""I am Kim Woo. Admiral Windsor has confirmed me as the cabin boy on the St. George. Due to his recent incapacitation and the typhoon, I have not received the paperwork. I do hope you have.".”

""I have not. Hmm. Leaves us with a dilemma, doesn't it? Do you have experience?"?”

""Lots of wonderful experience, Sir, just none as a cabin boy or seaman.". I'm small for my age – going on fifteen.”

It was not a lie – in slightly less than 365 days I would be fifteen. So, although true, it had been a slight exaggeration.

The Captain laughed out loud and placed a hand on my shoulder. I figured that had to be a good sign. It was unlike everything I had ever heard about no nonsense sea captains.

He continued.

""Will your parents sign a release so you can sail with me?"

"I have no parents, Sir. The Reverend with the mission here will vouch for me if that will help."."

"Hmm. Fifteen, you sayHow old are you?"

"Going on," I said, wanting to keep the facts straight – technically.

He smiled at me again; "Yes, going on."

""You think I look too young? Remember, I am Chinese. We come in smaller packages than what you are used to."."

""You are a sly young man, Kim Woo."

"Perhaps, although I am sure you will agree the fact I am honest and dependable and would be your tireless servant will be more important than anything bad that , 'sly', might imply."

"You talk like a professor, son."

"I've been told that before, Sir. I love words."

"The admiral himself, authorized this, you say."

At that point I was slipping into repeating a blatant lie. I tried the 'side-step-the-issue-tactic.

"Yes, I did."

I figured affirming what I had already said made it more like one lie rather than two. I pushed on.

"Can you imagine a man his age galivanting high on the ropes? I didn't know him for long, but I did note he had an often demonstrated a need to show off. Perhaps, I should not have said that. If it was out of line please allow me to withdraw it."."

"No need for that. You have him well pegged. We need to speak of your duties should I take you on. Please accompany me to the ship. Will you need to say your goodbyes to anybody here?"

"No, Sir. Like I said, I am alone."

We approached a group of men standing close to the gangplank. Upon closer look, it was not just any group of men – they were the men from my village who had decided to sail to America and who had invited me to accompany them. Mr. Ling was with them. The Captain – his hand still on my shoulder –

spoke with them. Mr. Ling was the spokesman.

""We have paid passage to the California of San FranciscoMexican port. Your first mate took the money and told us to wait here while he had the captain Captain approve it."

The men studied me, clearly not understanding what was going on. Theyn went on as if they didn't know me. I responded in a similar manntcher. The Captain spoke.

"I'm sorry men, but you have been duped. The first mate for this voyage has not yet arrived. Somebody took your money and ran with it. I'm sorry, but no passage money, no voyage."

The men looked back and forth among themselves. I could see the sadness and disbelief taking its toll. The Captain urged me on ahead of him up the plank. I had another idea. The first was working out so well, I chanced offering it. I tugged gently at the Captain's sleeve, so he bent down, and I whispered in his ear. The conversation went back and forth for several minutes as we stood there halfway aboard. He turned back to the men and spoke again taking two steps back down the plank toward them.

"This is my new cabin boy, here, Kim Woo. He tells me you may know him – gives you all high references. I happen to be down a dozen seamen. Kim didn't exaggerate your experience – or lack thereof as the case seems to be – but attests to your character and work ethic. He further suggests I might consider taking you on as hands – you work out your passage here on the ship as we sail. Seamen have a rough life – on call twenty-four hours a day. You will age twice the days the voyage lasts. Die onboard and you'll be buried at sea. Have a surgeon on board who can handle the regular things from fever and broken bones to fire in your belly. No medical guarantees. Disruptive behavior gets you time in the brig and or flogging. Mutiny, or talk thereof, gets you hanged at my discretion. I will send somebody presently for your decision. Think hard about it."

I had been honest about them with him. He had been honest with them about the demands of such a voyage.

He and I moved to the top of the gangplank and walked directly – midship toward the rear – to a short set of stairs that descended below deck. We were soon in his quarters – rather fancy, with curtained windows across the back of the ship, which provided a magnificent view of the sea. There was even wallpaper and lanterns hanging from the ceiling and a colorful rug on the floor.

""Your wage will be ten dollars for the trip provided you do your jobs promptly, adequately, and without grumping."."

""Oh, Sir, I cannot take money. I need passage like the others from my village. I couldn't take anything they also don't get."receive."

""I see. Something for us to chat about later. Can you handle a long gun?"?"

""At this point I could certainly deliver one whale of a blow to a bad guy's skull by swinging one. I have confidence that I can learn their proper use with a minimum of training."

"I have no doubt about either of those. My only concern about you is that you will own the shipping line before we make port in San Francisco and fire me."

We chuckled together. Minute by minute I was feeling more certain I was making the right move – the voyage.

"My teacher said I was the brightest student in my school. In fact, he let me help teach the younger students. I am a very good cook and an excellent swimmer."

"Let's hope you don't have to swim. That is seldom an indication a voyage is going well."

We shared chuckles over that. My stomach became queasy – I had not given the prospect of disaster at sea any clear thought.

"We have a deal, then?"?"

"Yes, Sir. You can count on my best."

"Ask any questions of me or the crew during the first week. After that, I expect you to have mastered the ropes onboard."

At that point, I didn't realize the saying – 'mastered the ropes' – meant just that on a ship. From the deck up to the Crowsnest in seconds and the reverse in less than that. I would practice. I had always been strong and agile. The prospect actually looked to be fun.

"No special privileges. Expect for me to treat you like the rest of the crew. About my question, then – we still have a deal?"

"Yes, Sir – is that the proper way to address you?"

"It is."

""We have a deal. Thank you, again. You may have saved my life, you know."

He offered no response to my words. He did speak,

however.

"Go tell the men from the village what I have told you about life on the St. George at sea and welcome aboard those who agree to the conditions. One of my crew will help them settle in."

He motioned to a barrel-chested man laden with tattoos and scars and those seemed to be his positive characteristics. I would learn he was called, Tat. His smile reeked of suspicion – I had no idea what to do with that. I would need to deal with it, since there was no place to get away from it once we put out to sea.

"Another question, if I may, Sir. Do I salute and if so, to whom and when?"

"No salutes here in our quarters. Watch the First Mate and salute when and to whom he salutes. Once we leave port, we are extremely informal on the St. George. Often just too busy for such silly formalities. You will get to like the men."."

"Thank you, Sir. I will certainly make every effort to do that."

Deep down inside, I doubted his words. I doubted if there could be anything comforting about being stranded at sea with a bunch of overgrown men, naked to their waists, bearing tattoos from dragons and lions to nearly naked ladies.

I left to give my friends the good news. The big sailor, Tat, accompanied me. The new First Mate arrived just in time to jump aboard before the gangplank was raised. He couldn't have been more than a half dozen years older than I. The men from my village were pleased at the arrangement and, like the Chinese will do, overdid their declarations of appreciation.

I had a question for the First Mate, Mr. Mathers.

"How long will such a journey take?"

"Depends on the winds – direction and strength. Best case this time of year, thirty-five to forty-five days. Worst case, sixty."

A few minutes after noon, the crew raised the huge anchor. It was a far more strenuous task than I had imagined – chains the size of a man's bicep, ropes the diameter of my wrist, gears and brakes and gizmos I had no ideas about. It seemed every man onboard was tugging at the main rope. The anchor hung at the rear on one side, and I was told it weighed over two tons. That was as heavy as twenty-five or thirty men.

On the masts above, straps were untied, and the sails were unfurled, hanging limp and useless for just moments as if unsure what to do with their newfound freedom. Gradually, they stiffened and became one with the strong breeze. I couldn't tell if the sails were taking charge of the wind or if the wind was taking charge of the sails. It felt like magic as the massive vessel seemed to awaken from a long sleep and slipped out onto the ocean. It was clearly a joyous reunion among the wind, the waves, and the ship. People on the dock cheered and waved hats. It was wonderfully exciting. It was terribly frightening.

I got sick to my stomach. Tat, the big sailor with the naked lady on his right bicep, took me to the rail and rubbed my back as I upchucked. I appreciated that. I had noticed there were no 'please and thank yous' onboard, so I wiped my mouth on the back of my sleeve and gave him a heartfelt nod. He returned it with a broad smile. Those men might not be so bad after all.

Before long, the Captain's strong arms twirled the wheel to his left and the course, east across the Pacific ocean, was set. At that time of day, there were no shadows playing across the waves and within minutes, none of the familiar sounds of life ashore remained – just the gentle lapping of water against wood and the occasional flap of a sail, struggling to remain robust and full. Gradually, the smells of the land – many, of course, combined into a single smell I hadn't even realized existed – gave way to that of the ocean. It was simpler and cleaner – maybe fresher was a better term. Unlike on land, it was constant – never changing from bush to bush or street to street. It didn't seem better, just different. I wondered if that would become monotonous. I wondered if it took unpleasant smells to make you appreciate the good ones. I wondered if I would miss what had been left behind.

The first ten days were, like the Captain had suggested, were difficult – so many fully foreign things to learn and so little sleep over one continuous span. It was more like a series of cat naps throughout the day and night. And then, there was the language. A seaman's variety of English was spoken there – it was English and yet it was not. It wasn't that I couldn't learn it. It was that it wasn't a language – at least not the one I had spoken at the mission.

What I knew about sailing came from a lifetime of listening to the men at the docks and from a number of books I had read. It was my understanding that all ships leaving the country carried opium – the most profitable product. A single ship completely loaded with opium could make the captain Captain wealthy for life.

Such ships were, therefore, targets of pirates who typically attacked within one hundred miles of shore – let the big ships do the hard work of navigating the open sea and then board them near the end of the journey. The battles were often bloody. The pirates came into such a fight with a shipload of seasoned fighters who understood their share of one shipload of the substance would make each of them wealthy in their own rightway.

Knowing those things, I felt relatively safe during the first five weeks of the journey. By then, it appeared it would be a forty-day trip and I began sleeping poorly, wondering if we were in danger anywhere other than inside my head. I took to sleeping on deck, aft, above the Captain's quarters – as if that could in anyway stop anything bad from happening.

At midnight, one night, near the end of our journey, when we were setting about fifty miles off the California coast, the man in the crow's nest, atop the middle mast, called down to the deck. We had been sailing under a cover of low clouds. I was aft on the main deck and his voice had awakened me.

"Ahoy, below! Ship to port."

As if rehearsed, men appeared on deck and snuffed all the lanterns. Port was to the left as we headed due east toward the coast. With the moon slightly to the south of the ship, it put that other ship ahead of what moon there was. From time to time its silhouette could be seen – that was what the sailor had seen from up top.

The Captain was soon standing by my side at the rail, his long, brass, tele---scope extended and scanning the skyline to the south and west.

"There she is, boy. A better view. Take a look."

He handed me his telescope, itself a big deal I figured.

I looked. His eyes were better trained for such a thing than mine. I could tell there was a vessel, but he reeled off the make and size and tonnage, and possible cannon power. I handed it back. He spoke, mostly to himself.

"She's headed north, following a search pattern for low riding ships I assume. If she veers due east we'll know she has spotted us. Another hour will put us into the morning fog off the coast. Once into a thick bank we will turn south and be lost from her."

"South, Sir? Will that not take us closer to her?"

"I am hoping her Captain will assume that, also, so he'll believe we will turn north, following your logic."

The First Mate came and stood beside us.

"Our cCannons aft, Sir?" he asked.

The Captain nodded and the young man left to tend to it. There were only four cannons onboard – all of them on wheels and constructed to fire over the rail on the main deck. Many pirate ships were known to carry forty or more. We would be no match if it came to a fight.

The Captain called up-top.

"Call her course!"

"Seems steady as she goes. The air is all muckied up, Sir."

"Muckied?" I asked.

"Patchy fog. Interferes with maintaining a clear view. This far out, it comes and goes quickly. Unless an offshore breeze sets in, we should remain well hidden."

"So, are you saying we are safe?"

"Pretty much."

We kept to the same easterly course we had been on for days – the final adjustment, the Captain had said, before we came upon California. I was excited! I probably should have been terrified.

"Is there time for one question, Sir?"

"Always time for a question – the point always is, will there be time for a proper answer."

We exchanged smiles. With me, he displayed a playful nature. I never once saw it between him and the rest of the crew.

"The man up-top referred to ships 'riding low'. I don't understand."

"Empty ships ride high in the water – they weigh less. Ships that are loaded, ride low in the water – they weigh more. Seldom will a pirate go after a 'high rider'. No profit in taking an empty ship."

"Thank you. I assume we are a 'low rider' and therefore worth the picking."

"An interesting way to put it, but yes, you grasp the concept."

captain The Captain kept watch.

"It's turning, Sir," came the seaman's call from above – "east nor east."

That didn't sound promising.

"What, Sir?"

"Can't be sure. I can't see how it might have spotted us. My best calculation is that it's doing a routine change of course – a zigzag pattern to explore a wider path as it continues to move mostly north looking for prey. San Francisco is the most likely port for a ship carrying the sort of cargo they are after. If it is a pirate ship I expect it to keep on its new bearing for another half hour before turning back south and continue its search well out to sea. If it's Captain has spotted us, it would likely have doused all lights onboard. We'll keep a good watch."

"It's all so complicated. Tell me when it's time for me to become frightened."

He chuckled. I had been serious.

He motioned two additional seamen up the main mast each with a long telescope. The Mate and a few hands had moved the cannons into place and were securing them to the deck when the man in the crow's nest called down, again.

"She's gone dark, Sir – doused her lights, and has changed her course – heading right toward us like a fresh hound after a fox."

CHAPTER THREE
My Captain

"Quiet on deck! Man the big guns! Break out the long guns!"

It had been the Captain in hushed tones to the First Mate. I had already learned that sounds traveled long distances over calm water. Never had I seen so much activity carried out so quietly. He spoke to me. The men – most of them barefoot – knew the routine even before the orders had been passed on. Captain Higgins spoke to me.

"You should go below, son. Since I know you'll find a way around such an order, your job will be to make ready that lifeboat – the one amidship to starboard – and be the first in it should it come to abandoning ship."

He was correct on all counts – I would have found a way to stay on deck and I did need to feel I was being useful. Within minutes, I had the boat ready to drop if it were needed. Within just a few minutes more, we sailed into the thickest bank of fog I had ever experienced. Had I not known better, I would have braced for a collision. My hands disappeared just a foot in front of my facee. I could make them appear and disappear at will. It was such an odd feeling – knowing I was there but unable to see myself. I figured the sudden change in the weather was giving us a big break. Actually, of course, it was more a rearrangement of the weather rather than a change. Well, I understood the difference anyway. Although I could no longer see across the deck, I soon understood the Captain was at the helm – the big wheel that steered the ship. I felt it take a hard turn to starboard – right. He was following his plan – sailing back south. Clearly, the weather closer to shore at that time of day was no surprise to him.

Fifteen minutes later, he headed us back east – toward shore – approaching port at full masts. I had learned that was a signal ships often used to alert those in port that all was not well so emergency measures should be readied. If the pirate captain had seen that, he would probably have pulled up rather than face a cannon barrage from shore. I felt relieved – still nervous, but relieved. I had already learned he was a master of sailing the open sea – calm sea or raging sea. Now, I knew he was every bit as good during emergencies – no visibility while being chased by pirates who outgunned us twenty to onein every way. Never once through all of it did I detect so much as a tremor in his voice or hand. I wondered if I would ever possess such courage.

The breeze from the coast had picked up from the coast and blew the fog to wherever fog went when the sailors no longer needed it as a shroud. Moving into the wind called for tacking – a zigzag maneuver. That slowed the ship considerably but also kept us from easily being tracked.

Since dawn,s the sun had begun fighting its way through the remaining fog – 'burned it off' was the sailor's term – and it created short-lived, overlapping, rainbows and splashes of quivering color as if playing a game of hide-and-seek. As the fog lifted, it revealed a long row of huge wharfs spread out before us as if reaching into the sea to welcome all comers. I had never envisioned such a magnificent sight. There must have been fifty wharfs and more ships than that. It had to be San Francisco.

I trotted to the Captain's side, hoping he would have important things to point out to me. He had been my teacher all those months.

I asked, just to make sure.

"San Francisco, Sir?"

"Yes. It's some sight, isn't it, Kim?"

I looked up into his face. He always called me boy – short for Cabin Boy, I figured – so hearing him speak my name was something special. He put his arm around my shoulders and pulled me close – like a father might do on a special occasion, I imagined. We just stood there like that for some time taking in the magnificent sight. I didn't want to move from it. The first mate was maneuvering the ship for docking – needed practice I figured for such a young officer.

"I am not sure how to proceed now that we are here, Sir. Do I stay on board? Do I leave? If I leave, where do I go?"

"You are free to leave once the passengers have left. I suggest a four-part plan: locate the men who came with us from your village and make decisions with them; retrieve your box of personal items from my cabin – I will provide you with a soft leather pouch that will take up less space than the box, and lie flat inside your shirt. It will, and therefor be safer; make your first stop, Mama ChangAntonio's – a place to sleep and eat until you firm up your plans. She'll be good for answers when you need them. She and I are old acquaintances. I will give you the address; and finally, stop by the paymaster. He will want to say goodbye before your final trip down the gangplank.

"It has been a pleasure having you sail with me. I would encourage you to sign on permanently, but you are an intelligent bright and capable lad with aand there is a bright future ahead for you."

"Thank you, Sir – for the time here on the St. George and the kind words."

He gave me a hug right there in front of the crew and everything. I still have a hard time believing that. The paymaster handed me a pay envelope. I looked inside.

"Sir, there has been an error. The Captain and I agreed on ten dollars American money for the journey. The envelope contains twenty."

"The Captain knows you pretty good, kid."

"What do you mean?"

"He said you would balk at the extra ten. There is a note from him in there."

In my puzzlement, I read it out loud: "Master Kim. For your services above and beyond the duties required. Take it! That's an order, son."

I smiled.

There was a second note folded separately. 'To whom it may concern regarding the character and work ethic of Kim Woo. He has acted as my personal Cabin Boy from China to San Francisco. I have never had better. He worked with precision and seldom had to be prompted – never reminded. He attended to his duties professionally and was a joy to have in my life. Signed, Captain Higgins. _________

I smiled a smile that returns, even today, whenever I think of it. Twenty dollars was more than my mother ever had at one time in her whole life.

I talked with Mr. Ling and the other men. TheyWe had learned that the the new, transcontinental railroad – twenty-five hundred miles of new track – railroad was being laid in two main sections – one growing west from a state called Iowa in the center of the country, and another east from California to eventually meet it in a territory named Utah. It would take several weeks by stagecoach to join up with the one coming west, but it paid better than the eastward section. I had other reasons to believe that was the one for me. The men opted for the one from California. They were in need of immediate cash. I would travel across the mountains by stagecoach and hook up with the west-moving crew in the Wyoming Territory (at that time, sometimes still called the Dakota Territory).

The men from my village had agreed to work the ship for free passage. The Captain arranged for each of them to receive an amount equal to what had been stolen from them, earlier. He was a fine and fair man – not to say they had not earned it. They had!

My first meal at Mama ChangAntonio's was the familiar food I had been raised on – rice, pork, noodles, and tea. It felt like home – a welcome change from the diet of beans and salt pork on the ship. I lingered there savoring it and the oriental decorations and music. I would miss the sea. I would miss the crew. Most of all, I would miss my Captain.

Initially, the man at the stage office was reluctant to sell me a ticket. Although I was well into being fourteen at that point, compared with American kids, I looked twelve or so. His reluctance may havelso partly been because I was Chinese. That had never been a problem for me – being a young Chinaman in China! I smiled. The Captain would have enjoyed that.

I learned that Cheyenne Town was a journey of 1,800 miles on poor roads across California, Nevada, Utah, and the Dakota Territory, and that the fare was 1½ cents a mile plus food. In fact, it would take something over a month. Such a trip would exhaust my money. I just couldn't imagine myself siting still for that long. My mind went to work on the problemshifted into high. I had done it before and managed an eight-thousand-mile ride at no cost to me. Why could I not do it again?

"Do you carry help on the stage runs – repairs, care of the horses, and the passengers and their belongings?"

"Just the driver and shotgun."

"Shotgun?"

"Like the armed guard to discourage highwaymen and big cats."

None of that seemed good. Still, I continued.

"I understand that I would not be your first choice for such a position – although I am very good at caring for wounds and fevers."

"What position? There is no position. You are making up something that does not exist."

I went on, ignoring his protests.

"I could keep them in water and sandwiches. I could also entertain them; I was the best Erhu player in my village. I played with others in a small orchestra. I do not have the instrument with me."

Something about all that seemed to catch his attention.

"Can you fiddle?"

"I know of the instrument. I assume I can learn. I learn fast. Would you look at a recommendation from Captain Higgins ---- of the HMS St. George?"

Before he could 'no thank you' himself out of it, I produced my note for him and flattened it on the counter. He was willing to read it. In fact, after he skimmed it in a goodhearted, if insincere, gesture, he adjusted his glasses and reread it, apparently, with interest.

"What would you expect in pay, being young and inexperienced as you are?"

A negotiation seemeds to have begun. That was usually all I needed. It had always been said I was quick of mind and good with words.

"Two meals a day and water as needed. I will do tasks as directed – always without question. I am good with tools and have spent time repairing things made of leather. People say I am likeable and make excellent conversation to help make the time pass quicker. I know dozens of wonderful Chinese stories I am sure the passengers have never heard."

He reread the note and looked me over.

"Can you lift that keg of nails in the corner?"

"I sincerely doubt it, Sir. I can lift relatively heavy carpet bags and sacks of oats, and one end of a trunk, however – more likely actual needs on a stagecoach than nails."

"I'll make you a deal, son. The coach leaves in three days. You work around here with me during that time and prove you can be useful. If you can do that, I'll put you on as far as Carson City, Nevada. That's about five hundred miles. You will ride up top when the coach is full and when the paying customers are uncomfortable around Chinese. It'll be up to the drivers from then on. You will be adding to the expense of the run. Not sure how the owner will react to that. That will be on me."

"Perhaps more expense, but the additional comfort I will be supplying will more than make up for it. I predict that within months other stage lines will be following your lead – adding a third man to do the bidding of the passengers and ensure their comfort. A former cabin boy should possess all the required skills."

"You actually make good points – like a luxury train run."

I still had some unfinished business.

"Do those three days here include meals? Clearly, if I am working here, I cannot work elsewhere to earn money for food."

He smiled at me and agreed. He understood my game and was willing to let me play it. I liked the man. Apparently he liked me. In truth, I had seldom met anybody who didn't!

"And a place to sleep, perhaps."

"Up over the stables out back."

"One more question, Sir. What are the chances I will be accosted while sleeping?"

"Accosted?"

"Sorry. Chinese. It means put upon, waylaid, harmed, robbed."

"Oh, yes, that accosted," he said, not wanting to appear unschooled. "I can guarantee your safety."

Early on, I had noted the English I had learned from the missionaries was many cuts above that which was spoken on ship by the crew. It now seemed that it was also better than the English speakers in America. Another smile – three of them in as many minutes. That just had to reflect good things about this America.

"Then, I accept your offer. I begin at dawn tomorrow. Will I need to find American clothes?"

"No. The city is crawling with Chinks – sorry – that was rude – with Chinamen."

I neither accepted his apology nor argued it. I had endured some of that from crew members on the St. George. I always let it go, like it was nothing out of the ordinary to me. I had more important things in my life than showing how hurt I was by such unpleasant wordsthings. They only hurt deeply if I let them. I didn't – well, sort of. It was more difficult to overlook such hateful wordput-downs when they were directed at friends or associates. I knew I was a great kid! I was getting better at holding my tongue toward those who hadn't recognized that yet. Grandfather had said, 'It is their loss'.

"One thing before I leave; where can I watch and hear fiddlers?"

"Martha's, Penny a Dance, just up the street. Tell her Buck sent you."

"I don't understand the name of the establishment."

"Lonely sailors come to town after making port. At Martha's, a man can enjoy holding a woman close on the dance floor for a penny a dance. Such feelings probably haven't arrived in your life yet."

"I assure you that my feelings are larger than my stature, Sir. I am not a child. In the morning, then. I am looking forward to demonstrating my skills. If I take a liking to the coach business, I may just own the line in a few years – and Martha's long before that."

"With the coming of the cross-country railroad, the stage lines will soon be things of the past, son. They will put us out of business. Progress, I suppose. You look to the railroads for your future, not the coachestrains."

I nodded as my way of thanking him for his advice. It was, in fact, probably very good – soundly thought through. I was interested that the cost of holding a woman on the dancefloor was the same as threequarters of a mile when riding a stage.

I spent the rest of the day walking the streets and learning about my new home – America. I took in Martha's place and expressed my desire to learn the fiddle. I also enjoyed looking at the pretty women all dressed up in fine clothes.

One of the men took time to show me the basics of the new instrument – they were similar to the skills used on the Erhu which *only had two strings rather than four. Both used bows. It would actually be easier to play than my instrument once I got the hang of it.*

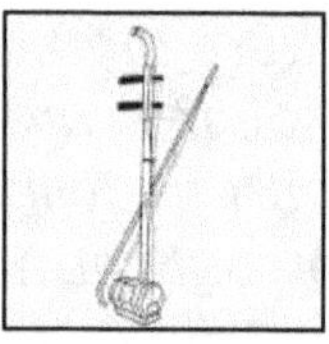

ERHU

Marty, the ship's cook had prepared a small bag of food for me – he had tossed it to me as I left down the gangplank. "Travelin' food," he called after me. I waved a big 'thank you' to him. He returned it and wished me well. We had grown close. Several others had similar words for me. They were an uncouth, motley crew, but most had treated me well and would have laid down their lives to protect me had the pirates boarded the ship. That is a rare quality in men.

I found a grassy area several streets inland from the ocean, made myself comfortable in the shade, and enjoyed the first few moments I had found to relax. Everywhere I looked was something new to me. I saved half the food for later. The aroma and mix of flavors kindled good memories. It had been a full day since I had slept, and I suddenly felt very tired. I closed my eyes and did not awaken until early afternoon.

Earlier, I had passed a store that sold musical instruments. It was hard to imagine that there would be such a place right there in the town where I lived. Back home it was a three-day walk to a city. I returned to the store. With food, lodging, and transportation arranged for the next month, that meant I had some extra money. When I opened the door, a small bell tinkled. It was nice and felt friendly. I looked up to find it. It made me smile. For just a moment it reminded me of the big bell in the tower of my school back home.

"I am interested in looking at a fiddle – an inexpensive one, please."

The man took several from the shelves and lay them on the counter. He talked about features but never price. Eventually, I settled on a used one – strong strings, tight pegs, with a bow made from fine looking, blond, horse mane. He tuned it for me and showed me how to do that for myself. The total came to three dollars. He threw in a stick candy – thinking I was a youngster –

an advantage that often worked in my favor like that.

Once back out on the wood-plank sidewalks, I headed for the stable that was to be my home for the next several days.

Almost immediately, I saw that I was being followed by a man who, although I could not identify, seemed somehow familiar – an unpleasant situation. When I sped up, he sped up. When I slowed down, he slowed down. He was tall and slender. I figured I could outrun him should it come to that. If needed, I'd head for the roofs where I could jump from building to building and surely lose him. Nearly every building had a ladder running up the side at the rear. Something related to handling fires, I was told.

I let him draw near. Hoping to get a better look, I stopped and leaned back against a building. He did the same, trying to be inconspicuous. When it came to tailing somebody, he was the most incompetent tail I could imagine. Why he had not approached me I didn't know but from his behavior, I doubted it could be good. It gave me a few moments to study him – tall, strong, and thin, like I said. Maybe a new haircut. There was something else. Although his forehead and ears were well-tanned, his cheeks and chin were pale. Had he been hiding his face behind the bandana of an outlaw? I had heard stories about such a breed of men in the west. More likely, I figured, he had recently trimmed off a beard. Who might do that? How about a sailor fresh off a ship. Perhaps off my ship? Perhaps that was why he looked familiar. None of that helped me identify him, however.

At last, he turned in my direction and began casually closing the gap between us. A well-dressed man passed me, headed in the direction I was heading. Like most men there, he wore a handgun in a holster. I had also heard stories about that and actually being right there with way too many to count made it seem even more extraordinary.

Hurrying, I sidled up next to him and spoke in a low tone; "Please do not look behind us but there is a man following me and I believe he may have bad intentions toward me. May I walk with you to the end of the block?"

"Of course. Can you describe him?"

"Tall and thin, bBlack pants and vest and boots with fancy, silver spurs. His shirt is dark green."

"I saw him – a sailor making like a ranch hand."

"I don't understand, Sir."

"Dressed like a cowpuncher so he'll blend in, but his legs are straight – not bowed like a horse-riding, cowboy. Walks like a girl in those boots. Have yYou hadave a problem with a sailor?"

"Not that I know of. Was recently shipboard from China. I had no problems there, however."

"You been showing cash around?"

"No. I bought this fiddle earlier in the day. That pretty much wiped me out, I'm afraid."

I did not want to reveal my financial situation even to this apparently nice man.

"Where you headed, lad?"

"To the sStage office. Just got hired on there."

"Good luck. Day labor is not easy for . . . Chinamen, in these parts."

Before I could thank him for his words of wisdom, the man following me called out.

"Hey, Yellar Boy. Come here."

I knew the voice – Salty John – from my ship – one of the worst – spent two weeks in the brig for cutting another sailor up with a knife over an extra piece of bread at mess The man I was with and I turned at the same moment. I did. Salty John had pulled a gun. He was clearly not well practiced. A shot sounded. His gun dropped to the street, and he called out in pain. Hise hand was bleeding and he held it close. He had dropped to his knees in the street. What shooting.! I had certainly selected the right man to sidle beside.

A tall, wide-shouldered man wearing a badge appeared as if from thin air. He and my man exchanged a few quiet words, and my bad guy was put in handcuffs and taken away.

"Oh, my, Sir!"

It had not been a great come-back to the events, but it was all I could muster.

He turned to the man who had protected me.

"That'll be all, Deputy. I will walk the lad to the station."

He turned back to me.

"Do you have a safe place to stay the night?"

"Buck, the station maste,r, allows me to use the stable – loft, I suppose it is called."

"He's a good man. Let me fill him in on what happened."

He opened the door and motioned me to enter ahead of

himme. Buck greeted him with an open hand and big smile.

"Marshal Keating. I see you've met my newest hire – Kim Woo. He is about to help me start a new tradition of luxury on our line. I have great faith in him."

"You heard the shot, Buck? Somebody looking to do the boy harm. Just wanted to make sure he made it back to you safely and that you understood his circumstances."

"Thanks, Marshal. We can handle it from here. My men won't let a hair on his head be damaged."

'Marshal', I thought to myself. I really had made a good choice for a walk-along-buddy – first a deputy and then the Marshal.

The big man with the big hat and big smile looked down into my face.

"Sorry for the unpleasant reception you got here in my town. Not the usual cordial San Francisco, 'Hello'."

He looked at Buck.

"You warned him about the problems of being Chinese here in the west."

"I have, sort of. I'll clear it up."

"You listen to Buck, Kim Woo. He's a wise man. Do you need anything?"

"I have everything I think I will need. Clearly, I don't know your western America well enough to know if I have everything."

The Marshal offered a smile and his hand for a shake – my it was a big hand – the handshake was something I was not used to since it was not a part of my culture back home. I managed. The big man left.

I detected an immediate problem; the Marshal indicated 'his town' was usually a cordial, friendly place; he also indicated that warnings about personal safety needed to be given to Chinese new to the town. Friendly and dangerous. Now that, I didn't understand.

"Better eat, Kim. See Cookie in the green building."

He pointed to the back door.

"Yes. Thank you, I will and thank you for your many kindnesses."

"I will leave 'Coach Line Identification Papers' with the head driver in the morning. They are valuable so guard them well. They will be good for any telegraph message you may need to send and

will identify you if you should ever need that."

That evening as the sun closed in on the horizon out to sea, I made my way up the ladder in the stable and found a comfortable looking place beside a large, open window. I watched from up above through the cracks in the floor to learn what I could – the basics. I had no experience with horses. They were exclusive to the middle and upper classes in China. I had spent time tending to oxen back home. I supposed that would transfer.

It was a much larger operation than it had appeared to be from up front – four large stables back there, with many horses and a dozen coaches. There was also what I learned was called a bunk house where the drivers and hands slept, and another with twin chimneys, which was where the food was prepared and served day and night at a long table with benches – much like it had been on the ship. My samples suggested it was both varied – unlike on the ship – and tasty. What had been 'mess' onboard, was 'grub' there in the west. I remembered when it had just been, 'mealtime Kimmy', back home.

I spent a whilesome time getting acquainted with the fiddle. I soon had it figured out and felt comfortable with it. There would be many hours of practice ahead before I would be comfortable playing in public. I needed to learn American songs.

I formed a nest in the hay and was ready to curl up for the night. By then, it was dark inside the building. I set my head to be up and at things by dawn. All in all, I believed it had been a good first day in San Francisco: I had met the Marshal, the bad guy was in jail, music was back in my life, and my tummy was full. I slept well.

I was awakened by the sounds of men downstairs. I tucked in my shirt, slipped into my shoes, hurried down the ladder, and watched the men to understand what was going on. Clearly, 'the crack of dawn' was earlier in the West than it had been elsewhere in my life. Buck spotted me and walked over. One thing I liked about the American West – nobody seemed to be in a hurry – everybody always had time for each other – for me. They all took my questions seriously – that made me feel important.

"Breakfast chow in the mess hall," he said. "Eat your fill and come to the front office and I'll get you started. You sleep well?"

"I did, thank you."

Those next three days were exhausting – before sunup to

after sundown. I had no idea how much work went into keeping a stage line running. More than 'hitch 'em up, drive 'em, and unhitch 'em' for sure. By dark each day, I was ready for sleep. On the ship, I had also been busy all day, but my duties there were not heavy on the physical side – lifting, climbing, and so on. It was more carrying messages, managing the inventory, keeping the Captain's quarters spotless, and helping the cooks serve at mealtime. The one similar thing between them was the huge amount of food the men put away. They stopped eating not because they were full but because time ran out. Everything ran on schedules. That was brand new to me.

I enjoyed washing and brushing down the horses when they pulled in after a long day on the trail. They clearly enjoyed the attention. I enjoyed the work, although I would not want to make a life doing those things. Horses seemed more magnificent from a distance without the close-up odor. My mother had said every situation in life had useful things to teach me if I wouldwill pay attention. Thinking back on the previous severaltwo months, I had, indeed, been taught many things. I figured that as I began facing life ahead all by myself, I would have many chances to let life prove just how useful those lessons would be.

CHAPTER FOUR
The Judge Called my Name

I learned from the men that traveling east by train to the construction head would be many times faster than by coach, but I had free fare and food on the stage and no money for train fare. I was in no hurry. Well, a boy my age was always in a hurry, but I had no personal schedule I had to meet.

Those next three days passed rapidly. I was impressed with how quickly I was catching on to things. My goal was to handle the team – hold the reins and snap the whip. I was told I'd need to put on another fifty pounds before I wanted to try that. After some reflection on the task that made sense, although at first hearing it, I was terribly disappointed.

Finally, the big day arrived. By six o'clock that fourth morning we were traveling east out of the city and into the sun. It was an extra fancy, extra wide, coach behind six powerful horses. I pitied the horses – they had no alternative but to look into the sun. It was a surprise to be riding behind a six-horse team. Most of the coaches I had seen come and go were pulled byonly had four. It was something about the strain of traveling the mountains, I figured.

Chuck was the driver and Amos was riding shotgun. We were carrying four passengers – all well-dressed adults – two women and two men – all under forty, I figured – none of them were related as far as I could tell. I had heard nothing about why they were headed east on the stage. The coach comfortably fit six adults. They were traveling together as far as Carson City,

Nevada – nearly six hundred miles. Chuck said that because of the mountains it could take two weeks and pretty well get us over the most rugged terrain. I had never seen tall mountains so was looking forward to it – quite a change from both my home back on the plains of China and my journey on the flat, endless, Pacific Ocean where some days, even the smallest ripple was cause for celebration.

Things went well during the first week. The team was changed several times a day at stage line outposts, called Stations. Driving the stage was no easy matter. Aside from handling twelve reins at once, it also seemed to call for swearing at the team on the way up the steep slopes and riding the brake with similar words on the way down to keep the stage from overtaking the horses and pushing them off the road from behind.

At about noon on the first day of the second week, as we rounded a curve atop a fairly high hill, we were put upon by a band of outlaws, standing in the center of the road and brandishing weapons. I was riding in the cargo rack at the rear of the coach. With so few passengers there was little to stow back there, so I had the right half of the leather cover open – top to bottom. It made for a comfortable ride if you didn't mind seeing where you had been, rather than where you were headed. Each had its advantages.

The leader of the group — a fat, dirty, greasy looking, little, man with an over-sized hat, and a huge, black, moustache – called out to the driver.

"You have a Yellar Boy on your coach. ? You will hand him over to us. Our client needs him immediately."

That didn't sound good for me if Chuck obeyed the man or for Chuck if he didn't. The bad man – who seemed to be a middleman of some sort – continued talking in some foreign accent – Mexican, I would learn later.

"While you are doing that, your passengers will hand over their valuables – jewelry, money, everything of value."

One of his men produced two canvas bags.

"You have bad information, Sir. There is no boy onboard this coach. We are carrying four adults who have ridden with us since we began the run in San Francisco."

I was sure Chuck figured I had overheard the instructions and had skedaddled to safety, so when the coach was searched,

I would not be found. He was counting on the passengers not giving me up.

I had been given no training for such situations – robberies. In fact, as I recalled, such things had not even been mentioned. The first thing the shotgun did was toss his rifle to the ground. It made me question why he was riding with us if he made no moves to defend us. They liked me. I should be okay.

The highwaymen were afoot on the road and had not seen me. I slipped down onto the road at the rear of the coach and tummy crawled into the tall weeds alongside the road. The question in my mind was, 'Where were their horses?' I went to look and soon located them just on down the hill a bit – ten tethered together on a rope tied between trees. From the looks of the area, the men had been waiting for us for a number of days. The horsesy were saddled and ready to ride. Many had rifles in the leather scabbards hanging from the side of their saddles.

First, I gathered those guns and hid them in the grass. Then, I led the horses back up the hill that held the road we had been traveling. At the top, I got them trotting at a good pace, to within sniffing distance of a creek, and let them go. They continued down the hill and across a meadow to the water. Something I had once read in a story prompted all that. I returned to the stash of rifles, picked up two of them and crept back to the coach. The thieves had their backs to me at the rear. I managed to catch Chuck's eye from the stand of trees where I was hiding and showed the guns.

He motioned to me – forming his hand into the shape of a six-shooter the way boys did, pointed it into the air, and made like he was shooting it. He pointed to me and nodded.

The outlaws had, by then, moved the passengers outside and relieved the women of their jewelry and the men of their guns and wallets. They were busy going through their bags. That had busied them while I was receiving my signals. I carried out what I figured Chuck meant, firing repeatedly into the air., I selected the trunk of a fallen tree and took cover beside it and opened fire. I added my own twist and fired into the trees, snapping small branches above their heads hoping to make it seem there was a larger rescue team. I was not familiar with firearms, but the branch thing had worked so well to distract and confuse them, I fired at the gunnysacks they were using to collect the passenger's possessions. The men dropped them, one having been hit in the arm. I felt badly about that. My plan had only includeding scaring them away empty handed. Clearly, I had been successful in making them think there were several firing at them. They dropped their gun belts into the dust.

They had soon turned and were running toward their camp tether line. Watching men running in western style boots was quite comical. Once they were out of sight around the bend, I rushed onto the scene and shouted. 'Into the coach. Chuck, get us out of here, now!' I tossed the second rifle to Amos – the Shotgun – and did what I could inside the coach to calm the passengers. Amos tossed the gun belts up onto the roof of the stage and took his place on the seat beside the driver.

Chuck soon had us flying down the hill. I poked my head out the window and made further explanations to him – that they had no rifles or horses. I believed we were in pretty good shape. One of the men passengers had thought to toss the two bags of valuables into the coach before he climbed back aboard.

There was lots of nervous laughter – not sure it could really be characterized as laughter. Chuck pulled the coach to a halt at the bottom of the long hill. We took a few moments to gain our composure and drink. We then continued on the way at a less hectic pace. There was much chatter among them about the encounter.

"Up here, Kim!"

It had come from Chuck. The driver on a stage was like the Captain on a ship – the boss! I crawled out a window and climbed up to the seat beside him. I spoke first.

"I hadn't been told there would be a dangerous adventure thrown in during the ride. Will that be deducted from my pay?"

"I swear, Boy, if you ever do something like that again, I'll tan your hide. I don't care how old you are. You could have got yourself killed, child."

"Didn't, now, did I?!"

"Yes, I see that. Actually, it was a great plan. You saved a good deal more than the woman's trinkets and a few dollars from the men."

"The coach you mean. I figured that was my responsibility as an employee of the stage line."

"No. What you didn't know was that under the floorboards,

we are carrying a lockbox full of gold – three months' payrolls for both the east and west bound railroad workers – several thousand dollars' worth. Out here, dollars are worthless – everything is paid for in gold. No gold, no whatever you want to purchase. I'm sure there will be a good-sized reward in it for you."

"I guess I don't understand why. Wasn't I just doing what I am being paid to do?"

"We'll let the owner of the stage line determine that. I'll report the incident by telegraph at the next stop – a couple of hours on up the road."

Figuring that conversation was over, I moved on.

"I like riding up here, Chuck. It makes it seem like we are moving along at a tremendous speed – like it did standing up in the crow's nest of a tall ship. That was an unbelievable feeling. Nothing but sea in all directions. I heard there was a brand-new train engine that a few months back went as far in one hour as we go in one day. Can you believe that?"

"It does seem unbelievable – fifty miles in one hour. I'm thinkin' any faster than that and the human body would just fly apart."

First, we came upon the west to east work-head and twoa weeks later the second – the one working west from Iowa. I asked around the first site for word about the men who had come with me on the ship. No one seemed to have any information. They were not mine to take care of, but for some reason I felt responsible for them. I guess I was like my mother in that way – it seemed she took care of our entire village.

I stuck with the coach until we met up with the westbound work crew.

As I was preparing to wave the coach on its way without me, Chuck removed a small, drawstring, pouch from his vest pocket. He tossed it to me.

"From the owner of the line – that reward I said would be coming to you. Don't show it around. Been good knowing you, boy. Take care of yourself. You're a teenager and that means you are still reckless. I know I can't stop that, but I can warn you of the certain danger there is in being a thoughtless male your age. Be more careful than you have ever intended to be before. Good luck!"

Bless his heart – he cared for me and did the best his words *could do to let me know. I had no way of knowing the truth in what he had said.*

He flicked the reins gently across the backs of the horses and moved out of my life. Even the snobbish passengers waved to me as they passed. I watched the trailing dust for some time. I felt alone, really alone, for the first time since I left home. A well-dressed man in a white, western, hat walked over to me.

"I'm Fletcher – Fletch – and I'm the crew boss for the railroad. You lookin'g for work?"

"I may be. Told you pay top dollar."

"For good help. Laying track ain't easy, especially for a small one like you."

"If you employ Chinese men, you know size is never a consideration."

He tipped his head left and raised that shoulder as if yielding my point.

"You don't talk like a Yellar Boy."

"I suppose you could call me an educated, Yellar Boy."

"Sorry about that. It's just what your kind is called out here. I intended no offence. What can you do?"

"I am a pretty good cook, I served as cabin boy on the HMS St. George under Captain cc Higgins-----, I am very well organized, get along with almost everybody, am trustworthy, loyal, give a dollar's effort for a dollar's pay and I am told my fiddling is improving every day."

He broke a smile and pointed at my fiddle, where it was clinging to my backpack.

"You'll have a chance to show your skill evenings if you want to. Your kind usually engage in their own sort of music, however."

"Just wait until you hear our kind ofthat music calling out from your kind of a fiddle, Sir."

"I look forward to it."

"I'll take you on for a week on clean-up detail. If you work out well, better things may be in your future. If not, I'll send you back to base camp on the supply train.

You job description is simple. If it can't be used but can be burned, burn it. Direct horse and sled teams in to pick up the rest. Once there are passengers riding the trains, we want the view to be spotless. Got it?"

"Yes. Got it. It is actually a very good job for a boy with my talents. I like getting to prove my worth up front."

"Pay is twelvefifty cents a day. A few men like you (meaning Chinese, I understood), have worked themselves up to thirty centsa dollar a day – not many. No educated, well-spoken men out here. You'll likely be made fun of if you talk that way – like a professor. Chinese laborers must make their own way – shelter and food is not provided for you like it is for the whites. The Chinese generally take care of each other so become part of them`. Can't say I dislike any of them. Hard to get to know them – the language thing."

Mother would have called that a backhanded compliment. I would take it. I had experienced it before. It was accepted as fact among most white men that Chinese were inferior as a race and therefore were not due to be treated with respect and kindness – as human beings. I didn't understand that. Almost all of the bad men I had encountered in my lifetime, had been white men. I would study that situation.

I was concerned that somebody out there in my new world, was after me – and rich enough to pay others to find me. Maybe it was the man the marshal had dispatched to the brig – er, jail – back in San Francisco. I had no idea why he had ill-feelings toward me.

Kim handed the finished crutch to Mack and turned directly toward him.

"That is pretty much my story. I found this spot, near water, sheltered by trees overhead and a thicket of bushes on three sides. During the six weeks I have been here, I have done well with the work crew. They seem to like me so long as I stay in 'my place' – at least I get along with them. They're kidders – my color, my size, my words – but I can take it. I believe that for most of them they do it for fun and not for hurt – even though it does. Evenings, they ask me to fiddle for them. I am learning the songs they like. Because of my age, they do not expect as much effort from me as from the men. Although I make that work to my advantage, I try hard to demonstrate that I'm no slacker – I earn my pay every day. Fletcher regularly offers compliments about my work. I would say things are going quite well – as long as Bad Guy or his posse doesn't find me. Probably thinks I am too young to work the rail laying, so I assume he's looking elsewhere. I wish I knew how he knew I had beenwas on the stage. I suppose it was no secret especially after the gunplay with the deputy. I'm sure I was a novelty – being hired by the stage line so young and so Chinese. Such things get talked about. Word gets around."

The long evenings sitting alone have given me time to restudy the papers I brought with me. Up until recently, I had only taken time to scan them. Since they had to do with far off America, I had no way of dealing with them. They represented a fantasy, as good as if I didn't even really have them. They contain some very interesting revelations. It was one of those that prompted me to take the stagecoach trip east, and here I am.

"It has often been said that once Kim Woo starts talking, it is difficult to shut off Kim Woo's noise hole, Mackrk. I hope my long-winded story has not been too boring."

"Not at all, Kim. It was revealing and exciting. You are a natural storyteller and a very clever young man. I feel like I know you – know you *and* like you."

"Thank you. I am eager to hear your story, Macrk, but before that, how is your leg doing?"

"It hurts but no worse than I would expect. You took very good care of it. Keeping the two sections of the bones in line will be a very good thing. Thanks, again. Nothing required you to help me like that. From your story, I sort of understand how you have come to be like that – caring and helpful. A priest once said to me that a boy can never escape his mother's teaching. It seems to be true for both of us, I believe."

"My people believe that we must all take good care of each other, MarkMack. The lesson of history tells us when men stop doing that, mankind suffers; it withers and dies a terrible death."

"A good belief. I get the point, just haven't thought about things that way before, I guess. You clearly grew up surrounded by gentle, thoughtful, people. I, on the other hand, survived a childhood of hot-headed, Irishmen and all the people who hated us. I must warn you, I have never been a successful friend outside the Irish community. I hope things can be different between us."

"I hope that as well."

You said we needed to move from here. I'm quite sure I will be ready to do that come morning. Will you go to work?"

"We will see what is what come sunrise. The end of the rails is some distance west from here. Maybe it is time to find a new place to camp up there nearer the current railhead. I have been considering it. Earlier in the week, II found a spot that I think could work. We can investigate it tomorrow. I will skip work, I guess. I am eager to hear your story and see if we have plans to make together. So – your story?"

"I don't often tell it, because it doesn't paint all that good a picture of me – when told honestly."

"I am not here to judge you, Macrk. I just want to know your story, so I can understand about you. Please realize that no story is required from you if that will be too uncomfortable.

"Help me change position – maybe, scoot me back and lift my leg up a bit. I seem to have slipped forward."

"Sure."

They worked at it for several minutes.

"You need a blanket yet?"

"I'm fine. Thanks. Still a bit dizzy when I move my head quickly."

Kim rolled up a blanket for a pillow and lay back against it, positioned to easily watch Macrk while he talked.

Macrk took a big breath and began to speak.

Judge Burns was an older man with red cheeks clinging to a pale, long narrow, wrinkled face. It offered neither a kindly nor unkindly appearance. His long, white, hair touched the shoulders of his black robe. He made no effort to cover a small bald spot on the top of his head. From the moment he looked down from the bench and engaged my eyes, I knew I was doomed. I felt life slipping away and fought to keep my legs from trembling. Of the four of us boys standing there in front of him – I was the youngest.

"Mack O'Henry."

"That was me."

"Yes, Sir."

"Step forward."

I stood there frozen. Jack, my next older brother, who was standing to my right, gave me a push. I stumbled forward all quite awkwardly. I had already embarrassed myself and the proceeding had not even really started.

"You are the youngest of the lot. About to turn fourteen, so you will be treated as a child in this court. The others will be

considered adults. Will you please take a seat over there while I dispense with the charges against the older boys."

A man in a policeman's uniform showed me to a chair. He handled me firmly but was in no way abusive. Once seated, I didn't know what to do with my hands, so I sat on them.

"I see we have two O'Henrys and a Bryant – fifteen, seventeen and nineteen. Each of you has previously come before the court on an unimpressive variety ofvarious offenses – brawling, damage to property, petty theft. None of those has been as serious as this charge – committing bodily harm in the act of thievery. The court document charges that on JuneAugust 2nd, during the nighttime-burglary of the tobacco store of Hiram Hess on 23rd Street, the man was struck on the back of his head causing deep lacerations and bruises. He was rendered unconscious, and as a further result was laid up in bed for two weeks to recuperate. In addition, a sum in excess of twenty-five dollars was removed from the premises. Is that an accurate accounting of what transpired?"

William, my oldest brother spoke for the group.

"Yes, Sir. That is what happened."

"Do any of you wish to offer some justification for your actions – had Mr. Hess harmed or threatened to harm any of you?"

"No, Sir."

"Do you know the word, 'unprovoked'?

"Yes, Sir. We are hardcore offenders, but we are nether dumb nor uneducated, Sir."

The response caught the judge off guard, and he allowed a quick smile, immediately covering it with his hand.

My brother continued.

"We steal so our family of seven can survive. We are sincerely sorry for the 'unprovoked' attack on Mr. Hess. It was dark. He came downstairs wearing what, in the shadows, looked like a policeman's hat. We would have never hurt our friend, Hiram."

"I will accept your statement as a guilty plea and sentence each of you to two years in the New York State Prison. Good behavior and a demonstrated desire to improve yourselves may become the basis for early release.

"I remand you to the State Penal System. Please show them out, Bailiff, and arrange for their transportation."

He signed three sheets and handed them to the man with the badge.

At the door, Jack turned to the Judge.

"Thank you for considering Mack's case separately. You know how little brothers tag along after their older brothers even when they have been told to stay behind."

I appreciated his comment even though it wasn't completely true. He left with the others. The judge called my name again. The bailiff positioned me back in front of the large bench. From above me like that, in a black robe and with long white hair, the judge looked to be God himself sitting on his thrown. Surely I wouldn't faint, would I? By then, I understood the power he had. Just like that he had taken two years away from my brother's lives.

"I hope you appreciate your brother's plea on your behalf."

"Yes, Sir. My brothers are good people. My family goes to bed hungry most nights. William and Jack always offer part of their share so we younger kids have enough to stop our stomachs from rumbling through the night. I often cry myself to sleep for my baby sisters."

"Tell me about your family."

"My father died by the bottle when I was ten. Sally, my three-year-old sister had just been born. Father had been a dock worker from the time he arrived in this country as a young man. He married my mother soon after that. You have met my two older brothers. I have mentioned Sally. Sarah is four. My sister, Mary, is fifteen. She and mother took in washings."

"You boys have Irish names, but your sisters do not. Do you know how that came to be?"

"We Irish are terribly mistreated here in America. My father believed having to bear the burden of being Irishmen would strengthen the boys – toughen us, you see – make us ready to face the hard life he knew we would have. He tried to make sure his daughters would be spared that. They and mother use the last name, Henry, in a faint attempt at hiding their Irishness – that may not be a real word, Sir.

"I understood. You are clearly well educated. Will you explain?"

"Mother's Father was a teacher and prepared her to be a teacher. She also had one year of formal teacher training. William came along and mother was expected to stay home. She took it

as her mission to see that her children would be among the best educated in the city. I believe she succeeded at that."

"That suggests a family that offered you many advantages. How does it be that you find yourself standing here before me?"

"Being a well-schooled teen, does not put food on the table, Sir. With my father an undependable drunk during our youngerearly years and gone from our lives early on, we boys first did what we could within the law. We tried for odd jobs. Irish boys are not hired – you've seen the signs on business doors – 'Irish Need Not Apply'.

"As we kids got older, we became more expensive to keep – clothing, food, and such. Unable to get hired, and with the city Social Service Center doing what they could to keep from having to help the Irish, we fell into desperate straits. At first we only stole things that we figured would not really harm anybody – trinkets from rich people, for example. As our situation at home became more desperate, we got braver, took bigger chances.

"We usually 'worked' outside our neighborhood – many of the families there experienced the same terrible problems that we did. We would never do anything to worsen their situations.

"When mother got the fever and died last winter we became less picky about whom we robbed. Hiram was old and single, without anybody but himself to care for. He didn't need much to live on. He had a thriving business. Our plan was not to take so much as to really hurt him – just enough to see to the welfare of our family for a few weeks. We all felt terrible about what we did to our friend, Hiram. The older boys have always sought work. William went down to the docks every day, trying for any sort of job. Now, they are in jail, and I expect to be hanged since I'm the one who struck Hiram. Who will see to my sisters? You have just taken their sole source of support away from them."

"Unfortunately, that is neither the purview nor responsibility of this court. My obligation is to dole out punishment proportionate to the crime. I rely on the law and precedents established by other, respected, judges. None of that may seem fair, but that is how it is.

"Considering the facts as I know them . . ."

I interrupted.

"But after a five-minute conversation with me you cannot, of course, know the most meaningful facts, can you? I only hope *you treat non-Irishmen with more compassion than you seem to have for us. Sorry. I should not have said that."*

He looked down upon my face for a long period but did not respond to my contention. I couldn't tell if he were boiling with anger at me or being thoughtful about my remarks.

He began again, modifying his opening words.

"Considering the facts as I am able to know them, I hereby remand you to the Christian Training Home for Boy Children in Rockford, for a period of two years. You will be fifteen at that time. If you take good advantage of your time there, I believe you show promise of beginning a proper life. I wish you the best of luck."

"May I say just one more thing, Sir."

"I suppose."

"I need to send a message to my sisters that apparently the best way for them to be well cared for while we boys are gone is for them to break the law and be sent to jail. "

The judge swallowed hard.

A large man who never smiled accompanied me on the stagecoach ride west. I was in handcuffs. He was not harsh towards me, he just seemed to be humorless. Not two dozen words passed between us. Several miles into the day-long journey he removed the cuffs. He gave no reason. I didn't ask. I nodded. He seemed to understand it was my way of expressing my appreciation.

The woman who greeted me – no, who met me – at the Home, also failed to offer even the hint of a smile. She carried a thick, stick, nearly a yard long, which added to my impression she was going to show herself to beher picture as an uncaring person. You can always depend on an Irishman to offer his hand, a broad smile, warm words of welcome and share what he has. Clearly, none of these people was Irish!

CHAPTER FIVE
It Came Time for a Change

The sStick-woman, with sunken, the beady, eyes and graying hair twisted into a bun on the back of her headair, spoke in a harsh, nasal voice – unpleasant in every way.

"Your name?"

I wanted to ask why she needed to know that – I was known for my smart mouth. I didn't ask.

"My name is Mack O'Henry. I'm surprised you don't know that."

"One of those disgusting Irishmen in the making. Come with me. You need to see this."

I followed her down a wide hall to a door marked, MISS IMHOFF, SUPERINTENDENT. She pushed the door open and impatiently motioned me inside. She closed the door behind us. Another boy about my age was there. He had been sitting. As soon as she entered, he stood – stiff as a board. She spoke.

"Master O'Henry, this is Master Benson. He is about to receive punishment. Tell Master O'Henry what your offence was."

"I failed to put my pen down when my teacher told us to."

"And your punishment for that?"

"Ten swats, Ma'am."

I was amazed. Toln what kind of a place had the Judge sent me? What kind of a Christian was this Miss Imhoff who would beat children?"

"Master Benson, assume the position. You know it well."

The boy leaned forward, elbows resting on her desk.

"Count each swat out loud and make it loud enough for me to hear."

He closed his eyes, clearly expecting something he knew would be painful. The ordeal began.

"One, two, three, four, five, six, seven, eight, nine, ten."

By then Benson was crying. Actually, by five he had begun crying. I could only imagine how terribly painful it had been. The stick was as thick as a cane, and she seemed to enjoy making every swat harder than the one before.

"Stand up. Dry your cheeks with your handkerchief."

He did as he had been instructed. She pointed to the door.

"Take yourself to the punishment closet and remain there until I tell you that you can leave."

I could only imagine that being in something referred to as the punishment the closet was not a pleasant experience. I wondered how long he would be forced to remain there. He went to the door where he stopped, turned to face the woman, and said, "Thank you for correcting me, Miss Imhoff." He left.

Surely those words were a requirement. No boy in his right mind would thank the person who just gave him a beating.

She and I were alone. She directed me to stand in front of her massive desk, while she took her place in the chair behind it.

"It was fortunate you arrived when you did so you could witness the consequences of misbehavior. We have rules that you are expected to obey. They are posted in the dormitory. Address your questions about them to the other boys. No disobedience is tolerated. You have been sent here to be punished for the misdeeds that brought you to the attention of Judge Bruce. What was your offense?"

I wanted to say, "For putting my female teacher in a coma for mistreating me," but I didn't.

"Stealing in order to feed my starving younger sisters."

I had overstated it just a bit. She didn't flinch.

"There is never justification for stealing."

I had lots of things I wanted to say to her about her take on that, but I didn't. Like the judge, she seemed to care more about the rules than people's lives. In my experience, the world was filled with uncaring people like that, and I was one of those who had no say in it.

"Judge Bruce probably told you to expect early release for

good behavior and attention to your studies. He's a softy. Don't count on that. I have been Superintendent of the Home for 19 years and have never recommended a boy for early release. When a boy behaves, he is merely hiding his true intentions. Boys are filthy-minded scum and you Finns are the worst of the lot. [Finn, a derogatory slang term for Irishman – derived from Finnegan, the last name of many poor, and often troublemaking Irishmen from the docks of Irish port villages].

I could see that the school board had picked an outstanding person to be Superintendent – one just bursting with love, compassion, and Christian values. What had I gotten myself into – and I was willing to admit that I had gotten myself into it?

She pulled a velvet cord hanging against the wall behind her desk and a boy suddenly appeared from a side door.

"Master Thompson, take Master O'Henry to the dorm and get him settled in – blanket, pillow, nightgown, uniform, and stockings. You know the routine."

She turned to me. "As you have no doubt noticed, our boys wear stockings – not shoes. Makes them think twice about running away. Ten miles to the nearest settlement. I have never had a runaway returned to me that wasn't hurting – head to toe. The staff does not like to have questions asked of them. Do you have any questions?"

I figured there was only one proper answer to that – "No, Ma'am."

She scooted us off flicking the air with the back of her hand. In the hall, Thompson spoke.

'Welcome to Hell. Around the kids, I'm called Tommy. You?'

"Let's make it Mack."

"You'll be in for some kidding – new kids always are. It's worse for the Irish – you'll get the 'Paddy' and 'Finn' nicknames. Prepare for one of the older guys to try and pick a fight. After he throws a few punches he'll probably quit if you don't fight back. Don't resist it or you will be pounded black and blue – and if that happens, never tell on him. Miss Imhoff loves to dole out punishment to tattletales. Never object or she doubles it. Ten swats really hurts. Double that has made the toughest of the guys pass outfaint."

"Nice place you have here."

"It has been called many things, but it has never been called 'nice', I can assure you, and none of us claim it as 'ours'."

I nodded indicating I understood or, at least, had heard the words. Time would tell if I really understood.

"How long you here for?" he asked.

"Two years."

"Count on three, then."

"Three? I don't understand."

"She adds a week for every serious offense."

"What makes something 'serious'?"

'Her mood at the time, mostly. Best advice is don't give her any reason to discipline you and don't fight. Study the rules well. Know them by their numbers because she's likely to ask you what Rule 17 is – for example – and if you aren't right, expect extra duty, or something."

"Extra duty?"

"We all have jobs to do – duty. They rotate weekly – laundry, kitchen, housekeeping, stables, yard, and things like that. Since I'm checking you in, I'll put you on my rotation, so I can show you the ropes.

"Thanks."

"If she believes we are becoming friends, she will probably change that. Friendship is frowned on."

He hitched his head and directed me up a set of stairs. At the top, behind a door of iron bars, was a large, open room filled with rows of cots – almost the entire third floor, I figured. At a table at the front of the room he loaded my arms with my supplies – things she had mentioned and others. I followed him to an available cot near one of the many windows. He helped me make my bed – there were specific rules about how to do that – and get into the school uniform – white, long-sleeved shirt, underwear, black trousers and thick, white, stockings. He put my clothes in a barrel marked, TRASH. The end of them, I figured.

"In the winter we get an extra blanket, thick long johns, and cold weather jackets."

I wondered about 'cold weather shoes' but figured I would find out when the time came. Back home we never wore shoes in the summer and in the winter, never when we were inside. Shoes were expensive and needed to be saved. They were passed down from older child to next and so on. After the severe wear and tear from two very active older brothers, I often got new shoes – from the church charity basement. I felt fortunate about that.

Then, we walked to the back of the room. The door allowed entrance to the bathing room. Twelve tubs in rows.

"We're allowed two baths a week. Allowed ten minutes each time. Youngest boys use the water first and work our way up to oldest. Bathe, dry off, put on a new uniform, and get on with the day's routines. If you aren't used to routines, it will be hard at first. There is only one proper way to do everything, here. Never be late. Never be early."

Routines were mostly foreign to me – except the two hours mother set aside for schoolwork every morning and I looked forward to that. None of us would ever miss it!

"If you're not sure about something ask me. If I'm not close by, ask another boy. You'll soon learn which ones will be helpful and which won't. Lots of the guys here are awful people. A few will give you wrong answers just to watch you get punished. If you don't understand all that, you soon will suppose that makes sense, doesn't it. For the first month or so, just do as the older boys tell you to. I guess it's like initiation. They'll ease up, especially if they learn you're easy to live with. One of the oldest boys is Damian – he is to be avoided whenever possible – has no soul and often rages out of control. He works at being terrible and hurtful. Word is he killed a man with his bare hands.

"Just one other thing I can think of right off; Gerald is a snitch – you know that word?"

"A tattletale?"

"Right. He reports to Miss Imhoff regularly — like her spy among us. She gives him special privileges in return. We all know about it. He knows we know, but it doesn't change a thing."

"You have been helpful, Tommy. Thank you. Now what?"

"I return to my duty of the week, being the runner for Miss Imhoff – like her assistant I guess you could say. For some reason she has taken to me. You will join the physical fitness team. It really isn't a team – it's everybody doing exercises one hour every day. I'll take you to the back yard and introduce you to Mr. Hawn. He will treat you fairly, but don't try to stretch the rules with him. He'll come down on you like a hammer."

"There is so much to remember."

"If in doubt watch me. That will almost always point you in the right direction. If I'm not around, watch Bill. I like you, Mack, but don't expect me to back you up when it comes to punishment

or to defend you when you are being picked on. I'd get it twice as bad as you. Do you understand?"

"Yes. I do. I was raised on the streets in the slums of a city. It is how life was there. Again, thanks, and by the way, I like you, too."

During the following days I began to feel like I was fitting in. I couldn't be sure if that was a good thing or not. I hated the place. Why would I feel good about fitting in?

As it turned out, the thirteenth day of my time at the home, was also my birthday. Back home each member of my family made us a gift on our birthday. I didn't tell anybody about it. It was lonely. It finally sank in that I was still going to be there for my next two birthdays – three, if Tommy's prediction was correct. I had not yet felt the sting of Miss Imhoff's stick. I had made a real effort to follow the rules thinking to do otherwise would be foolhardy – not in my best interests, for sure. Hating a place and hurting because of it were two different things. The first I could not control. The second I could.

Midmorning, my group had just finished a run around the outside of the grounds – sticking close just inside the wire fence that encircled the grounds. It had been five circles that day and we were tired. I was sure it was a good conditioning exercise, so I was not one of the complainers. I tried to turn it into a good thing for me – one of those 'good things' to find in every situation my mother had often spoken of.

In general, things were going rather well – I was accepted by most of the boys, other than being called Finn I wasn't really picked on, and I consistently made the highest marks of anybody in my schoolwork.

Damian had not confronted me yet, and I hoped he had let that possibility pass. I had done some thinking about how to handle him if he came after me in some way I just couldn't ignore. A guy had to have some lines he didn't let bullies cross. We were resting near the back fence – some were sprawled out on the ground and some standing, most were chatting. I was standing alone, leaning against the high, woven, wire, fence. He approached me and purposefully brushed against me – shoulder to shoulder – handing me a good jostling. I stepped out of the way, willing to let it go.

A few minutes later, it happened a second time. Then he

pushed me, hard. I ended up on my back on the ground. I stayed down until I was sure Mr. Hawn was watching from where he stood, twenty yards away. I took my time getting to my feet and approached Damian slowly but confidently until we were nose to nose. The other boys pulled back encircling us, waiting to see me get beaten to a pulp, I assumed. Allowing not a second to pass after we were toe to toe, I fired one blow to his stomach with my right hand, putting everything I had into it. Back home we called it the 'plex' – one powerful blow to a guy's solar plexus – the spot immediately below the breastbone. As I understood it, like the jaw, it had nerves leading to the part of the brain that turned consciousness on and off. His hands still at his side, his knees locked in place, his eyes rolled back into his head, and he collapsed onto my feet – out, stone-cold. I had seen it done several times but had not really considered I would ever use the move.

Mr. Hawn moved in – taking his time, I noted. The boys moved aside, clearing a path for him and expecting him to direct awful punishment for me. He knelt down and gently slapped Damian's face in an attempt to awaken him. It didn't work. He just lay there, limp, struggling to breathe. Presently, Mr. Hawn stood and motioned for two of the larger boys to pick him up with directions to take him to his cot in the dorm and stay with him until he came to. Miss Imhoff stormed across the lawn in our direction – Tommy was right behind her.

"What is going on here, Mr. Hawn?"

"There seems to have been an accident, Miss Imhoff. The way it appeared to me, Damian, here, tripped over his own feet and fell, awkwardly, hitting his head, which knocked him out. I suggest we let him sleep it off in the dorm."

The other boys looked back and forth at each other in astonishment. Jaws actually dropped.

"Very well. If you say so. Odd, though, wouldn't you say?"

"Oh, yes, Miss Imhoff. Odd, indeed!"

The two of them followed the boys back inside. The rest of us remained there by the fence. The guards smiled as they chatted about the event.

The moment the door had closed behind them, the boys surrounded me and let up a shout that I'm sure was heard for a mile in every direction. They crowded in around me offering slaps to my back and non-stop words of congratulations and admiration. Even her spy-boy, Gerald, joined in. He caught my eye and zipped his mouth shut. I figured I would be safe from the stick. Interestingly, I immediately became the hero – the Number One as the toughest boy was called.

What I had done was inspired by William, my oldest brother. His advice went something like, "If you find yourself in a strange group of guys and you feel trouble brewing in your direction, take out the biggest, meanest of the lot first, then the others will leave you alone." It was a terrible way to have to make a point, but in life-and-death situations, you have to think of your own welfare. I would talk it over with Tommy, later. It was the one time even mother had sanctioned retaliation – unprovoked violence against you or your loved ones. It was a boy's way of life where I came from.

I began noticing it that evening during dinner. It was Mack this and Mack that – Finn and Paddy were gone from my life. There was a second thing – Mr. Hawn was treated with respect – no words of disrespect behind his back – "Yes, Sir, ." "No, Sir, ." "May I help you with that, Sir,?" "More mashed potatoes, Sir?" – treated in a way he had never received to my knowledge. 'Tripped himself', my old shoe! Suddenly, we all felt we had somebody on our side.

Several interesting things occupied my mind that night as I waited for sleep to come. I had gained the boys' respect, even if not how I would have hoped it would have come; I had turned fourteen, and amazed myself with the power of my right hand when propelled by the force of my newly developing biceps; I no longer needed my brothers to protect me – I could do it myself; and, I had decided to runaway – to retake my freedom.

Unlike the Judge's hopeful speech, nothing the home had to offer me suggested it was the place to learn the skills I needed to make it out in the world. There were plans for me to make – careful, creative, foolproof plans. I would share that with nobody, not even Tommy. I would take whatever amount of time it took to make ready and execute the perfect escape. There would only be one chance – I understood that from my first moments with Miss Imhoff. It was like my newfound self-confidence had expanded my chest, straightened my backbone, and widened my shoulders. I awoke a new young man. The kid in me had been shed. It was *such a powerful feeling – a safe feeling.*

I decided that once I left, I would take a new name and shake the problems that always followed an Irishman. After some thought, I decided on the simplest route – Mark Henry. I was surprised that leaving Mack O'Henry behind caused a momentary shiver of sadness to run through my body. It wasn't fair – to have to give my name just because it was Irish. Maybe it wouldn't have to be forever.

I spent the next several weeks studying every aspect of the routines there at the home – the guards' assignments, the deliveries, work details, and such. It all pointed to one thing – the only time for me to make my break was by the dark of over night – the darker the better. Problem. There was a guard in our dorm all night – nine o'clock in the evening until six o'clock in the morning. The job rotated between two men. I made a point to get to know them. Every day I'd spend a few minutes with them, being friendly, earning their smiles and chuckles – really, earning their trust.

Several months passed. I continued to work out the details. Then, the big night arrived. I had managed to get assigned to 'dorm duty' that week. It amounted to one boy remaining in the dorm all day, keeping the dorm clean, the cots in proper rows, and rotating the sheets once a week. It gave me access to the storeroom where the sheets, pillowcases, towelstowels, and such were kept. I managed to confiscate several sheets and tear them into strong strips, tie the strips together and make a 'rope', which I could hand over hand down from a third-floor window on the south side – the backside – to the ground. There were no bars on the dorm windows – third floor – seemed reasonable, I figured – who'd try to jump twenty feet to the ground. That morning I had told the guard – Robert – that the next shift guard – John – had asked me to ask him if he could switch the shifts that began on Thursday evening for the one on Friday. He said yes – he'd let John take it. I told him that I was to report back that it was fine. In reality, I would not tell John, so neither of them would show up on Thursday evening allowing me the necessary, unsupervised, time to exit the window and make it to the ground. I announced to the boys that Mr. Hawn said the guard was going to be late arriving that night but that he expected us to follow the rules to the letter.

I arranged my escape to take place during the dark of the

moon – no moonlight. I waited until all the boys were asleep, tied the 'rope' in place, and made my way to the ground. I had positioned a thin, sharp blade at the end of a string that also hung to the ground. When I pulled the string from down below, the blade cut into and weakened the top knot and with a couple of tugs, the 'rope' of sheets tore and dropped to the ground. One tug and the razorblade followed. That left no evidence of how I had escaped.

Once safely on the ground, I rolled the strips of sheets into a tight package and made my way with it across the lawn to the stable, where I buried it in a trench I had previously prepared, then covered it in dirt and floor hay. The horses were housed two to a stall. I opened all the stall doors. I set ajar the outside doors just enough that when a horse pushed against it, it would open. All of that was to make sure none of the horses were harmed once I had started a fire in the supply room. I spread the coal oil from a lantern over the hay covering the floor and set it afire. While it was still not much more than smoldering twigs, I led a big black stallion through the darkness and beyond the fence to the west.

From the time I left my cot to having mounted my 'black' outside the gate took no more than five minutes. None of the individual boys could get in trouble because none would know about it. They would all still get punished, but it wouldn't be severe – a few extra laps, perhaps. Knowing I had escaped would be a really big deal and the boys would gladly take whatever the consequences might be. It would be one act of rebellion that would be seen as a win for all the boys.

I had stashed a sack of supplies – clothing, water, food, a length of rope, and other things – and had picked them up from the stable as I left. I had decided to put on the reins but not take time to saddle the horse, so I was riding on the saddle blanket. That had not been a good plan. The blanket scooted here and there. City or country, all boys knew how to ride, of course. I had to chuckle when I found myself planning how to do it all better next time – as if I figured I would be caught. Let's not have that, please!

'Black' and I kept to a walk as we moved on through the darkness. A running horse at night made sounds; sounds sent the wildlife scurrying and that made more sounds. My goal was quiet. After several hours on the run, it came to me that I was thirsty and hungry, and still wearing my nightgown, so we stopped, and I led the horse into a stand of scrub along a tiny stream. There should *still be several hours before I would be reported missing. I let him drink his fill and tied him there while I dressed. I sat on the blanket, broke open the sack of supplies, and enjoyed an early breakfast – not real early, it seemed. The dawn was breaking across the eastern horizon behind me. I had lost track of time. That would make it five-ish – still an hour before time to rise back at the home.*

Suddenly, I realized that I had not thought – planned – any further than the ride west from the stable into the dark. I'd be an easy mark as the world grew light. That was okay; I was a smart kid; I'd figure something out. Note to self: Next time I must plan out the first full month ahead of time! I smiled!

'That something, better arrive soon,' I thought to myself. Coming straight after me out of sunup were four men, riding straight toward me riding at a brisk gallop. How could they have found my escape so soon? How could they have followed me?

CHAPTER SIX
Escape to the West

I gathered my things into the bag and moved with them and Black further into the thicket. I had one biscuit left and put it in my palm and my palm up to black's Black's mouth. Horses didn't whinny while eating. I couldn't chance a whinny.

The men were riding four across as they drew closer. Their gallop was steady but not strained. They sat easy in their saddles. Their gaze kept to straight ahead. They passed within ten yards. Black nuzzled my hand and his large, rough, tongue made short work of the crumbs that remained there.

Several things became clear. The first was that they weren't looking for me – they didn't look from side to side as they would do if searching. They were not expecting trouble because they were neither startled nor distracted by the rabbits darting out in front of them or by the waving of the young branches standing firm to conceal me and my mount. I didn't recognize any of them as being from the Home. Regardless, I remained as still as the pebbles beneath my feet.

Within a few moments they had passed. All that remained was the low cloud of dust dirtying up the dew-dampened grass, as it settled back to the ground. Never before had two minutes seemed like twenty. I must have stopped breathing because I remember beginning again. I managed a long, strong hug around Black's neck. He allowed it as if he understood that for some reason it was important to me.

We resumed our journey with the blanket beneath me doing better than before, and the sack of supplies cradled between my legs at the base of Black's neck.

Presently, we topped a ridge. I pulled Black to a stop. It was a magnificent view. I could see for miles up and down a long, wide valley. There was a stream and a well-used, east to west, trail that shadfollowed it. To the far east, something was stirring up a substantial cloud of dust – cavalry, maybe; a six-horse stage or line of livery wagons? I couldn't tell, but my imagination always spun interesting possibilities. As a runaway, I was not yet ready to reveal myself to anybody. I tied Black to one end of my rope so he could graze. I fastened the other to a lone apple tree, picked a shiny red one for myself, and bellied down, wriggling forward on my elbows throughin the tall grass until I reached an opening. Spreading apart the grass ahead of meFrom there, I could watch the trail and the goings on down there. The position of the sun in the sky and shadows along the ground suggested it was no later than seven o'clock. The boys would have known I was gone. I still had most of the day ahead of me. I needed a plan. How about sprouting wings and soaring down to join the dust maker – whatever it was?

My city, Chicago, was one of the largest in the country. It sat on the southwest edge of a huge lake – Lake Michigan. It was all I had ever known. The boy's home I had escaped from was half a state to the west of my city, sitting just outsidein a much smaller town called Rockford, which sat on the border with Wisconsin to the north. I had thoughtfully opted to run toward the west – fewer people and more opportunity for me to get lost in its fabled vastness. The upside was, I was free. The downside was, I had fewno skills that would sustain me in the frontierout there. It was hard to win a fight brandishing [waving] one of Shakespeare's books in somebody's face. I was used to hard-rolled, graveled streets, clean, red-brick sidewalks, and an abundance of stores that provided everything I could possibly need. Where I was at that moment, certainly was not Chicago.

I could learn.

As a younger child, I had dreams of becoming the Captain of a big boat on the lake, but such a boyhood dream seemed less likely at that point in my life. It was just Black and me, and as far as I could tell, Black had no plans other than enjoying the shade and nibbling on the damp green grass while enjoying the occasional fallen apple. His needs seemed far simpler than mine and yet in their own ways, no less important than mine – survival.

There was a sudden turn of events down on the trail – the smaller, leading edge of the long, narrow, stream of dust suddenly left the trail and veered right toward the hill – my hill – my position. I raised up onto my knees in the tall grass to better keep watch. I hoped the presence of Black and me out there all alone alone would not seem suspicious. I hoped we wouldn't be seen. Back in the city there were always people around – most would help if it were needed. Unless the sitting rabbit several yards to my right would offer me his magical powers, I was in this alone.

It was a horseman on a small, light colored, horse – a pony, perhaps. It/he/they hurried up the slope in my direction. As it came closer I could make out more details, including that the larger trailing dust cloud also left the trail and followed, by then a hundred yards behind. The single rider wore no hat – extremely unusual under what, in several hours would become a blazing hot sky.

Oh, my! It was an Indian in buckskins and moccasins. I had seen pictures. My heart jumped. He wore a headband with a black feather rising from the back. Closer, yet, and I was able to determine it was a boy about my age. Several shots were fired up the hill in his direction. Things were getting serious. He lay forward, flat against the pony's neck to reduce his silhouette – make him less of a target. The idea of a half-dozen men pursuing and shooting at a boy on horseback seemed all quite unfair. I had to make a very important decision in the shortest momentsecond of my life.

When he gotcame within twenty yards of me, I stood clear of the brush and waved my hat above my head to draw his attention. He saw me and veered slightly away from me. I beckoned him toward me with sweeping, full-arm, motions. He looked back and forth between me and the men. I freed Black's tether from the tree and led him deeper into the stand of scrub oak that stood just a bit back down from the top of the rise. In there, we would be momentarily lost from the horsemen's view. I attended to picking a safe path among the stones, not looking back to see if he were following. If he weren't, there was nothing I could do about it. If he were, there was a good chance I could save his life.

The ground and tall grass were still wet with morning dew, so Black kicked up no dust as he walked behind me. Presently, I heard the hooves of the large group of horses slowing as they approached the top of the hill. That was to be expected, of course – tired horses. I stopped and turned to see if the rider had taken my suggestion and followed me. He had. Ten yards behind me, just into the thicket, he stopped and slid to the ground. I raised my hands. I wasn't sure why. Probably to show I was neither armed nor had bad intentions toward him. Following my lead, he did the same and offered a quick nod and smile. From what I had heard and read about Indians, I never thought I would be smiling at one. He was not yet close enough for me to see his face clearly. His attention rightfully remained on the bunch that was chasing him.

I continued to beckon him toward me trying to suggest that speed would be a good thing. He nodded and hurried with care in my direction. I knelt, motioning him to do the same. The grass was a good two feet tall – the Illinois version of prairie grass. We were both completely hidden. The two horses met and stood quietly together. It was a fine quality that horses had – meet and be friendly right from the start. People could take a good lesson from them. The pony had worked up quite a lather and was still breathing hard. Black nuzzled her as if to offer reassurance things would soon be better.

The boy was squatting in front of me watching for the riders to appear. The horses were standing behind me. The men in pursuit were a dozen yards in front of us. I was yet to really see his face and wouldn't until the horsemen had passed. Another near escape. I hoped such good things came in sets of at least three; I had suddenly used up two that morning.

He turned and there we were, our faces no more than a foot apart. I had never seen a real, live, Indian. I was surprised that his skin was a beautiful tan – yellow-tan. From the description I'd heard, I was expecting some hue of red. It was confusing, but that was clearly not the time to discuss it or give it further consideration.

"I sure hope you speak English, Friend, because once we get beyond 'up', 'down', and come here in sign language, I've shot my entire Indian vocabulary."

Unexpectedly, his face blossomed into a wonderful smile, and he chuckled.

"'I speak pretty good whitemanwhite man talk. Was tTaught at a boarding school nearly five days ride south of here.'"

"'I don't know of the school. Hello. My name is Macrk. I also have men chasing me – not so close, however.'"

He pointed to his chest.

"'Yellow Feather.'"

I suppose I smiled.

"'I would have guessed, 'Black Feather' I said, pointing to his headband.'"

He nodded.

"'It is my – what is your word? Skise?'"

I figured I understood – 'disguise'?

He nodded and smiled – "'Disguise'."

I wanted to laugh, figuring as disguises went, that must have been the worst I had ever seen – a yellow feather to a black one. I didn't.

"'Where are you headed?' " I asked.

"Toward safety,' " he said without hesitating.

It appeared to be his full answer, and it appeared to be a very accurate one.

That didn't suggest a destination, but I fully understood.

"Me, too. I ran away."

"'I run from rope.'"

He placed his hands around his neck – I figured I understood – hanging. I wouldn't ask more. He hadn't asked more of me.

"'I am heading out west,' " I said.

"'I go to find my people in Iowalowa Country,.'" he said.

"'I will pass through there on my way west to California.'"

"Maybe we go part way together, he said.. "I am good hunter. I am strong for age. I never speak badly of the Great Spirit. I share what I have. Most people say I have a pleasant, gentleness about me."

He spoke white man's talk very well and had certainly hit all the points of a good resumé. For some reason that seemed humorous.

"'Are you not interested in why men chase me, Yellow Feather?'"

"'If I knew, would that change anything about you or your past?'"

"'No, I suppose not.'"

"'If white boy men need to know about my past, I tell you.'"

"'Interesting. A minute ago, this white boyman needed to know. Suddenly, I don't. You presented a good lesson. I need to focus on this moment and what is just ahead.'"

Yellow Feather nodded but remained perplexed as if he could not understand why, by my age, I would not have already known that. I had been taught that white men were the smartest men in the world – perhaps that had not been the truth. With my new friend, I would be able to study about it.

I did have one more thought about Yellow Feather's past.

"'My only interest in your past is if there are things I would find helpful in case the angry riders return.'"

"'It was said I stole six horses from farmer. Those men say punishment is hanging. Do you need more?'"

"'No. I assume you'll let me know if there are other things I need to know. I will do the same for you. In my case, I was guilty of the terrible deed I was sentenced to jail for. You should know that before you choose to ride with me.'"

"'Do you plan to do such terrible deed to me?'"

"'Of course not. I have always been a good person.'"

He shrugged. The matter was apparently over.

"'I am hungry,' he said. 'I always get hungry after being chased for miles across the prairie.'"

Hmm! Perhaps there was more I needed to know. It sounded like being chased for some reason was an everyday occurrence in his life. He seemed older than he looked.

It was the first time I thought abouthad noticed his knife in his belt and his bow and quiver of arrows hung across his chest. Perhaps that was a good thing, because by then, I did not feel threatened by themir presence.

"'You stay here with horses. You chose good spot for camp. I move back to clearing and make sure men are gone. Then I hunt meal for us. You can build small fire?' "

"I can."

He was trusting me with his horse. What if I trotted off as soon as he was out of sight and went to sell her? It was a special feeling to know he trusted me just like that. That, of course, was all about him – being a trusting person. I had not yet proved it of myself, which would have been about me. I would prove that his faith in me was not misplaced.

I had sense enough to keep the fire small – big enough to cook some sort of small game but small enough to keep the smoke minimal. I felt like a real frontiersmanpioneer – well, until he returned just a few minutes laterr with his take. He had bagged and cleaned a good-sized rabbit and a very large bird all within ten minutes.

I didn't understand his first action. He kicked my fire out.

"'I say I am sorry for not instructing you better, new friend, Macrk. Please, let me say why.'"

"'Sure. I want to learn.'"

He cleared away the sticks I had set in place and built up a dirt circle eighteen inches across and ten inches high into which he re-set my kindling. He found four rocks, each twice the size of a small melongrapefruit. He searched the ground and pointed to a large flat stone – I had heard it called slate – like the blackboard Mother used in our classroom back home. It was the circumference of a barrel lid and about the same thickness. He relit the fire from a lingering coal, and with his direction the two of us set the slab of slate on top of the smaller four rocks – one at each corner.

As it turned out, Yellow Feather was a good teacher, which may have suggested he had had good teachers.

While he prepared the rabbit and pheasant – the name of the big bird, I would learn – and placed them on the slate, he had a question for me.

"'Remember smoke from your fire – tell about it."

That was certainly not what I was expecting from him.

"'Well, it was white and rose high in a single column. I see what you're getting at. This fire comes out all around the slab and just filters up into the air like a lacey curtain – it can hardly be seen. Small as it was, the thick, single stream of smoke from mine could have been seen for a mile or more. Thank you.'"

"'Did you know to use dry, soft, wood?'"

"'No, it was what was here. Why?'"

"'Wood that is hard or damp makes dark smoke, easily seen during the day. What rule does that make?"

"'Well, let's see. Use dry, soft wood for daytime fires – white smoke – and, I'm guessing, use damp, hard wood at night to produce dark smoke that won't be so easily spotted against the

darkness of the night sky.'"

"'You are smart student."

"You are a good teacher."

"Do you know about numbers?" He asked, again not a question I was expecting.'

"'Doing sums, intos, and times – things like that, you mean?'"

He nodded. I nodded.

"'When there is time will you show about them?'"

"'Of course. It will be a good trade between us..'"

I had the idea that my new friend was also going to be a "smart student'student'. He was a good hunter and cook, I could say that for sure. With his knife he dug some wild tubers – small, white potatoes and wild carrots and onions or scallions – and worked them in and around the meat as it cooked. It smelled like mother's kitchen. He even carried a pouch of salt.

I rehearsed inside my head:

'Let's see, dry, soft wood for white daytime fires and damp, hard wood for dark, nighttime fires. Mother always said to review new information immediately, so I wouldn't forget it. That was also fascinating – even though Mother was gone, a part of her lived on there inside my head – and inside my heart, I figured; after all, I had taken considerable risk to help the boy – probably saved his life. Mother would have approved, and those things made me feel good about myself.

Although, I was not accustomed to eating off the land, so to speak, the food was delicious, and I was actually full by the time we playfully fought over the few remaining carrots. After just those few hours, I had come to like, 'Feather' – the name I'd given him inside my head. Presently, even that would be shortened to, Feath. After all those months with the boys at the home, I had come to like very few of them and trusted even fewer.

"'Time to move on, I suppose,' " I said. "'Which direction?'"

"'The valley down there soon winds west. I turned east up this hill. My problem was back to the south."

"Mine was to the east," I added.

"Then, I say we follow the valley on west,'" Feath said.

"'That fits with my plan. You think those men will really keep looking for you?'"

"'Not sure. The leader is pretty bad man – Johnny Mason.

He wears black Stetson with silver band and has large, black mustache, big nose, and harsh – gravely – voice. I am quite certain he is the one who stole the horses. He was the first to accuse me of it. Out here, Red Skin always gets blamed first and people are willing to believe it without any facts. Mason rides brown stallion with over-brand.'"

"'I am unfamiliar with that term.'"

"'The original brand is changed by adding some lines. In his case, the Flying V was changed to the Flying W – like he doubled the V at the end. There are branders who specialize in that for cattle rustlers. They are called Refitters. One of the best of them lives just north of Boomer – the little town where all my trouble began. His name is Sam Waters.'"

"'They really hang a man for stealing a horse out here?'"

It had been my question to Feath offered with disbelief.

"'Hang man for stealing horse; send man to prison for short time for killing another person. Strange way of thinking about what is important. My people would never hang another human being.'"

"'I've heard some pretty bad things about what Indians have done.'"

"It is true but seldom undeserved. Not making excuses, but when the soldiers raid villages and steal the children and move them to special schools to take the 'Indian' out of them and make them white, braves from those villages have attacked them or burned the schools. I know there are other things, also. When your land is stolen from you and you are chased away, you fight back – Red or White. Just like there are bad men among the Whites, there are also bad men among the Indians.'"

"'I didn't know about such a thing – those schools and that Indian kids were stolen from their families, Feath." *

He smiled when he realized I had finally settled on a nickname for him.

"'I was one of the stolen kids. About six months ago, I escaped. I'm sure they are also looking for me. That school is five dayfive-day ride on south. I been riding north on Pony, here – friend provided her for me. It is long and complicated story. By any telling, it means I need to get out of this territory in hurry. Once my hair grows long again – they cut it like white men's – I will have better disguise.'"

I could certainly agree with that.

"'Don't you want to see your parents before you leave?'"

"'That is the first place they will look. The President's soldiers may have already torn our village down over it. I feel bad if they did. Regardless, my people would feel good about my escape. Villages can be rebuilt – a child who suffers at the hands of those schools can never go back to being who he was. They have probably moved on by now – my parents and brothers.'"

We headed down the hill, let our animals drink from the stream, and followed the trail west. When clouds of dust approached, we sought shelter in the hills and hid. There were very few travelers that day. Although Feath was eager to move on across what was left of Illinois toward the Iowa boarder, he set a leisurely pace saying we should save our mounts for emergencies. He did seem to know about emergencies, and I saw the wisdom in that. I found myself looking over my shoulder often. To say I was not scared would be a lie. I figured having two sets of men looking for us was worse than one set, but I understood I had a better chance of remaining free with Feath at my side.

We shared details of our lives as we rode – we became more open about our stories as time passed. By dusk, I felt quite close to him – comfortable with him. I believed the same was true for Feath. He was a year and some months older than I was. He had two older brothers – the soldiers targeted younger children to kidnap and take to the schools – easier to change their ways of thinking, I supposed. I shared about growing up on the city streets, being called Hey Finn by those who wanted to put me down, and other things about my family and upbringing.

Feath was impressed with my education and my family's dedication to learning. He was sympathetic about my mis-treatment, and he was understanding about my trouble with the law. Before we had stopped for the night, he had engaged me in helping him with numbers. He was smart – I supposed that would be expected of the son of the village chief. Leaders are usually smart – not necessarily, nice, but smart. One of his comments showed how smart he was, I thought. "What you call multiplication is just the upside-down of what you call division."

We located a private area near a spring-fed pond that was sheltered by a canopy of tall trees – oaks and elms and hickory. The animals drank. The two of us drank. We picked berries and apples for our evening meal and decided against a fire. It had been a hot day and would remain warm throughout the nighttime hours. If a chill developed, we each had a horse blanket that would keep us cozy.

"'Do you carry a weapon, Macrk?'"

"'No. I left packing pretty light.'"

'I will carve you a knife.'"

Feath had an excellent hunting knife – six-inch metal blade. He worked on mine while we continued to talk. I couldn't imagine how a wooden knife could be of much value. I had come to believe my new friend, however. If he said he'd make me a knife, he would make me a knife, and it would function like a knife. He took some time finding a piece of wood that met his requirements.

He talked about it while he worked.

"'Surprising, I suppose, that good knife can be fashioned from wood – hard woods like oak, walnut, maple, or hickory. I think oak holds the sharpest edge. When it dulls, just scrape it back into sharpness. With it, one can dress small game like rabbits and squirrels, cut rope, prepare fruits and vegetables for eating and things like that.' "

He was the master of fending for himself out in the unsettled world. I felt fortunate to have found him – or to have him find me – or us to have found each other. I often spent far too much time chasing such odd thoughts.

With the little blankets folded into pillows and the horses tethered for the night near the water, we said goodnight and prepared for sleep.

"'May the Great Spirit watch over you this night,' " he said.

"'Thank you. We Irish boys don't have anything that fancy to wish each other. Best I can do is, Good Night – see you in the morning.'"

"'I'm quite sure they mean the same thing. My grandfather said that from language to language, words are often more about feelings than meaning.'"

We had not been asleep more than an hour when it happened. I heard sticks breaking under somebody's hard-soled, leather, boots. I opened my eyes just enough to see that Feath was not there. My first thought was that he had needed to visit the bushes – after our day on the trail we had been pretty thirsty. It was more than that – his blanket was gone as if he had run out on me. It was too dark to see the horses. A person in moccasins didn't *readily break sticks as he moved across the land. I would keep quiet until I could figure things out.*

That wouldn't be the path things would take.

"'Turn over onto your back, kid.'"

The voice from above me was unpleasant – rough and hoarse – raspy. I did as he said. Where he stood, the moon lit his face – black hat with a silver band, big nose, black mustache, bushy eyebrows. It was most certainly Feath's bad guy, Johnny Mason.

------

*To learn more about the Indian Retraining Schools you might want to read another book by this author: Blue Fox: Boy of the Backwater Boarding School, written by Tom Gnagey, available on Amazon.com

CHAPTER SEVEN
Life with Feath was Never Dull!

"'You're not the Indian kid!'"

"'I've noticed that myself. What are you talking about, Sir? Indian Kid?"

"'I'm lookin' for a Indian kid about your age. Rides a pinto pony.'"

"'I guess that sinches it, Sir. I am neither an Indian boy or a pinto pony.'"

"'You got a mouth on you, boy..'"

"'I certainly hope so, Sir. An absolute necessity for the vital, precise ingestion of essential nutrients as well as scrutinizing innovative and relevant contemporary discourse on said topic.'"

I took some joy figuring that had seemed like a foreign language that left the man completely bewildered.

"'Stand up.'"

That I could do.

His tone had grown angry.

I figured me and my 'mouth' had pushed things about as far as I dared. I was facing him – my eyes to his Adam's Apple. He was positioned with his back toward the thicket as he continued to look over the camp. There was no trace of Feath – no blanket, no head band, not shoesmoccasins. Had he run out on me? I had so many questions and no answers. I detected something moving in the darkness behind the man. One of his men, perhaps – hidden backup?

Presently, that indistinct shadow behind him showed itself

– it was Feath. At that moment, he and I needed a plan. He had one. Through a quick series of gestures, he explained. He would slip a noose from his rope around the man's neck from the rear. I was to rush in and take his gun from his holster. We would tie him to the tree just behind him. It had been communicated with three very simple motions.

I hoped I had interpreted them correctly. Had it not been so serious, it could have been great fun – 'Pin the Bad Guy to the Hickory Tree'. I further distracted him by raising my hands as if in disgust at his behavior. I stepped a bit closer – close enough to be able to grab his gun when the moment came. I figured when the noose was tightened around his neck, he would immediately put his hands to his neck – occupying them – and he would be pulled backward a bit. I needed to allow for that in my lunge at him.

I took a careful step to my right – slow and deliberate. My intention was to confuse and distract him and turn him into the moonlight for Feath. The man mirrored my move trying to figure me out. That put his head and shoulders directly in the moonlight. It was at that moment that Feath raised the rope and dropped it in place. He drew it tight and pulled the man back against the tree. Surprised and panicked, he went for the rope around his neck just like I had predicted – I knew I sure would in the same situation – breathing would seem like a really good thing about then. I went for his gun with my left hand and pushed him backward by planting my head into his chest as I lunged forward. Feath was soon binding him to the tree.

"'Get the rope from his horse, Mack.'"

The man continued to struggle and offered a string of swear words that even I, a boy from the streets of Chicago, had seldom heard.

I soon had his ankles secured to the trunk. Feath pulled a handful of grass and made a ball of it, which he stuffed into the man's mouth to muffle his ability to call out for help. My friend added a few finishing touches – a rope across his open mouth and around the tree to hold his head in place and quiet his tongue. He removed the man's boots and handed them to me – I was still in stockings from the home. He opened the man's wallet and removed all but a few dollars, while he addressed him.

"'We are taking just enough to pay us for the inconvenience

you have caused us. We will let your mount go after we're well away. Probably borrow the saddle and bags for week or so."

By then, I had strapped on the holster, mostly because I didn't know what else to do with it – I needed my hands free. I slipped my good foot into the boot – not a bad fit – and transferred the saddle onto Black – another good fit, I supposed, because he offered no objections. I finished it off with a nice set of saddle bags – extra-large for long journeys.

Yellow Feather was still addressing Bad Guy.

"Because of the rope, you probably won't be able to spit out the grass. You might consider chewing it up and swallowing it. Then you wouldmight be able to call out and draw somebody's attention. Someday, I fully expect to prove you are the horse thief – two of your men told me they'd testify against you. It seems your associates hate your guts . . . Sir. That happens to bad guys."

Keeping an eye on him as we worked, we arranged our things to leave.

"Have a safe night, Sir. Haven't seen many signs of big cats so you'll probably be safe. Until later. See you in court. Hang in there, as they say!"

That had been my addition – it tickled Feath, and I was more than a little pleased with it myself. We mounted up, climbed the hill to the north, and descended into the valley on the other side. There, we came upon another fine trail and a small stream. Moving to another valley was Feath's strategy to throw the bad guys off our trail.

We set ourselves toward the west. It felt good to have a saddle beneath me and one foot in a boot. I still had my axe, rope and wooden knife. Feath had his knife and bow and arrows. I had added his revolvers and probably two dozen rounds of ammunition. I didn't want to keep the guns in sight so had put them and the gun belt into a saddlebag. Feath had taken the man's rifle and the sheath that carried it from his saddle. My quick, once-through his saddlebags, had found several boxes of rifle rounds. I wanted nothing to do with the guns. Feath seemed more comfortable with them.

I had questions for him.

"'What was that man's name, again?'"

"'Johnny Mason.'"

"'How do you think he knew where to find us?'"

"'That was my doing. I led us on the most obvious path – continued on the trail I had first taken. Should have gone some other direction – like over here. I didn't believe he would think I would double back like I did. I was wrong. He seems to really have it in for me. He knows I can have him hung. I suppose that might give purpose to him.'"

"'Why do you suppose he came after us alone?'"

"'Maybe his gang deserted him. Maybe they split up and are each searching different area for me, planning to meet up in day or so.'"

"'So, you're saying we still aren't safe.'"

"'That what I say, yes.'"

"'How did you know to leave camp?'"

"'Heard horse approaching and snapping twigs beneath its hooves. Believed I needed to become invisible and stand ready to help from behind.'"

"'It was a good plan. We left one upset gentleman back there. If he was angry with you before, just think how mad he will be with you after what we just did to him!'"

"'Oh, yes. What is word worse than angry?'"

It didn't need an answer. He made his point.

Feath became serious.

"'I think you should ride alone, Macrk. My problems with the man should not be yours.'"

"'Who says they should not be mine?'"

"'Your question is interesting. You seem to be saying what problems you choose to take on are your business and not mine.'"

"'Yes, and please don't forget that. Everyone must take good care of his friends.'"

"'Then, thank you for being my friend, Friend.'"

We exchanged smiles and for some reason eased our mounts into a gallop. I suspected that on my part that reflected my desire to get to safety and for his part to move me out of the danger he believed should have been his, alone.

I liked riding at night, sheltered from the sun's heat by the vast darkness and safe from prying eyes up and down the trail. I was tired and scared, but still, what I was doing seemed right for my new friend's sake. I figured by then, ol' Johnny wasn't really happy about me either. We rode on until we could see the mingling streaks of golds and reds of dawn working across the peaks to our left.

"'Tired?' Feath asked.

"'I am. I'm okay though. You?'"

He nodded and began looking around – for a place to stop and rest, I assumed. I did the same and pointed to a well-sheltered place protected by high rocks on three sides. Tall, old trees provided cover above and bushes across the open side up some five feet.

"'Looks good to me, MarkMack. We need to water the horses and wash away some of this dust from the trail.'"

He loosened the reins on Pony who turned south, directing us to a pond not 100 yards away. Given their head, that way, a thirsty horse will always sniff out the closest water. We dismounted and they immediately waded in shoulder high. The four of us enjoyed being in the water for a half hour. It felt good to be clean.

Before we headed back to our hideaway, Feath cut two, long, straight, sticks and sharpened one end on each. He showed me how to 'stick fish' – spear fish, I would call it. Before we slept, we had a feast of small fish. He asked me if I wanted to build the fire – it was a test, of course. I accepted. He smiled as he watched. It seemed I passed.

"'I will make Indian out of you before the week is gone."

I wasn't sure I really wanted to be an Indian, but it had been offered as a compliment, so I smiled and nodded.

We slept past noon. We felt rested – rested, clean, and full – well, not so full we didn't have room for apples and berries.

We were back on the trail well before mid-afternoon. We were sharing stories about how it had been for each of us as we were children, when a ruckus occurred on the trail some distance behind us. It was moving toward us rapidly. Instinctively, we both urged our mounts to our left up the side of the hill and found a place hidden from the trail. I stood tall in my saddle hoping to get the first peek at what was going on.

Short story: a covered wagon pulled by a team of four was being chased by two men. Bad story: There was no driver – it was a runaway. Good story: the men were firing over it – not at it. That seemed odd, but then I was a newcomer to such things in the west. I looked to my companion for direction. He handed me the rifle.

"'I know you hate this thing, but you need to lay down some fire in front of the riders as they come near. Kick up some dust. Get them to pull up. You ever fired one of these?'"

"'Never. I saw one fired in a Wild West show at the amphitheater, once. Doesn't seem that difficult.'"

Feath rolled his eyes. Clearly he knew things I didn't. He offered a ten second crash course in the essentials.

"'Keep butt of the gun tight against your shoulder or it may kick out and get away from you. Who knows what you might hit. I try to catch the wagon and stop it. I will return first chance I get. Just keep men from chasing wagon.'"

He handed me the rifle. He was right; I hated it. I took it, braced it like he had described, and took the first shot, surprised when they stopped, and the horses reared in place. I probably felt better about my skill than I should have. They looked around bewildered about where the shot had come from.

He offered several more words of advice, as he and Pony hurried off after the wagon.

"'Stay hidden. Move about. Don't let them get a bead on you. Make them think you are several shooters.'"

Not letting them get a bead on me seemed like a very good idea. I took one last look at the wagon. A face appeared just behind the seat – the face of a young boy on the ride of his life.

I moved from place to place. I spread my shots just in front of the men. My aim got better. They pulled to a halt looking around for me. They remained on their horses. I put the next two shots within a few feet of them, thenand urged Black back down the hill to the trail. Upon seeing me with the rifle, the men dropped their guns. I figured they had emptied them at the wagon. They had looked surprised when I appeared from out of the brush – my youth, I figured.   Unfortunately for them, they had already disarmed themselves.

I stopped withinpulled up five yards making threatening motions with the gun away. I must say, there was a large element of excitement about it.

"'Dismount. . . Kick the guns aside. . . Sit down. . . Remove your boots and toss them into the grass. . . Move three yards apart and lay face down in the middle of the road. Keep your mouths shut and close your eyes. . . My father and his friends will return once they have stopped the wagon."

My act even impressed me. They did exactly as I had directed. What power! THAT really impressed me!

I was a pretty good liar and hoped they took seriously what I had said. Let's face it, I was a great liar! I moved on them, confident as if I was armed with a Gatling Gun. Mother always said that knowing when to stop talking was a gift that God had failed to bestow on me. I held my tonguestopped, hoping what I had laid out would be enough. Where it had come from, I had no idea. Maybe a book. One of them moved his arms as if getting ready to get up. I fired again. It hit the ground way too close to him. I needed to be more careful. He didn't move again.

I remained mounted, thinking I had an advantage from above them. I wondered how many bullets the rifle held. I wondered what was taking Feath so long. I wondered what I was doing there at that place at that time with absolutely no plan for the rest of my life.

Several minutes later, Feath came back down the trail at a good gallop.

"'Need to tie them up," he said, dismounting. "They giving you any trouble?'"

"'We seem to have reached an agreement; they lay still with their eyes closed and I don't blow their heads off.'"

I couldn't believe I had really said such a gruesome thing.

Feath spoke at the men in the deepest voice he could manage.

"'Is that right – the agreement he just spoke?'"

"'Yes, Sir.'"

"'Yes, Sir.'"

They still hadn't seen him of course so didn't know he was another boy. He dismounted and used their neckerchiefs to blindfold them. That would maintain their belief he was older. We soon had them secured with their own ropes. I added their revolvers and ammunition to my growing saddle bags. We were fast becoming a mobile arsenal. With their arms tied behind their heads, we rolled them into the tall grass beside the trail. Feath had one more trick up his sleeve – well, not really – he was wearing a soft, loose-fitting, leather, vest.

He lay them on their backs, facing in opposite directions. We overlapped the lower halves of their legs – feet to knees – and bound them together. I thought it was an ingenious move. It would be impossible for them to stand or walk and there was no way to untie each other the way their hands were bound behind them.

He mounted Pony and hitched his head for me to follow. He explained as we galloped back up the trail to the wagon.

"'Grandfather and his two, young, grandsons. The old man owns trading post few miles on. They on way back from buying supplies to restock the shelves. The two men didn't shoot into the wagon because they figured it contained explosives. They know the store.'"

"'Are they alright – the boys and the old man?'"

"'Seem to be. The younger boy shows tears on his face – reasonable, I would say. When the men began firing, the animals bolt--ed and took to wild gallop on up the trail. The grandfather lost control of the wagon when it hit large rock. The old man fell from seat into the back.'"

We pulled up and dismounted at the wagon. The three of them were tending to the horses – calming them down. Everything was under control. We introduced ourselves all around. 'Pops', the grandfather, insisted we accompany them to his store to take a meal with him and the boys. It seemed to just be the three of them. We agreed. It was a small, well-kept building – they lived in the back.

First, Pop telegraphed a sheriff about the thieves and their location. They would be picked up within the hour. That made things seem much better in a hurry. I had lived among lots of really bad guys, but in the city, problems were solved with fists – not guns.

We were back on the trail within an hour, which was fine with me. The sooner out of there the better, I figured. Pop loaded us up with provisions like flour, salt, sugar and grease, and food and water – he insisted on providing each of us a large canteen. The boys ran alongside waving as we departed. Boys always did that. So had I. I wondered why.

"'Well,' " I began, "so far, my life with you has been one breathtaking adventure after another. Is this what I can expect?'"

"'Such things just seem to follow me. It could get worse. White boys are not supposed to be friends of Indian boys – both white men and Indians stick to that rule. It puts you in danger from most everybody as long as you are with me. Nobody ever explains why. Sometimes grownups can be very dumb – very stuck in their

stupid ways. Like I said, you should go your separate way. You will be safer.'"

"'And miss the great education you are providing free of charge? I don't think so.'"

"'You not receive my bill yet.'"

He held my eyes for some time, and we exchanged smiles. I had the idea he had never before had a whiteboy friend, so I would understand if he couldn't fully trust me. I supposed that worked both ways, come to think of it.

We chuckled on about it for some time. Life took strange turns. The west was a very different place from what I was used to – and I hadn't even really reached the true west yet. Word was, that started beyond Iowa.

"'Do you have any idea what you want to do from here?' " Feath asked.

"'Just before I ran away, an older boy arrived at the home, and he had stories to tell about a new railroad that is being built that will span the entire breadth of our country – Washington, DC in the east to California in the west. I have had some thoughts about checking that out – maybe getting hired on to help build it. Eventually, it could get me all the way to California. I'd like to be part of something so important."

"'Sounds like very hard work. You really want to work?"

"I figure I'd have to, eventually. Hard to stay on the right side of the law and not work to support yourself.'"

"'That is white man talk. When you work for somebody else, you help make them rich and you stay poor. Indians work just for themselves – hunt, pick fruits, dig vegetables, care for their animals, protect the land we all share – take care of family – live free. What is it about you people that has such a need for money? Indians have everything we need without it.'"

"'I have no idea. I must say, I haven't spent much time thinking about that option – possibility. I don't see how it could work – without money – in a city."

"'One reason Indians do not have cities, I suppose. Our elders say people do better in smaller groups.'"

"'I don't see any way we could change our way of life to be simple like yours, Feath.'"

"'You could if you chose to, of course.'"

He had a reasonable comeback, if not an answer, for all my responses so, I stoppdidned 't responding. I wasn't prepared for a debate. It was too huge an idea to adequately think through while moving west on a saddle through the tall grass all the while looking over my shoulder for a silver hatband on a man out to do me in.

Feath knew little of my way of life and I certainly didn't know anything about his. Mine had been comfortable but not without danger. His was intriguing. Both were scary in their own ways. Scary AND comfortable? Now there's a fascinating concept!

I was learning that getting to know a person from a different background was a good thing; it made me think about life in new ways – question the ways I had learned were right and wrong. Opening the door to new possibilities, improved possibilities, was a good thing, I believed, even if it was scary. It made me wonder just how many things about becoming an adult were going to be scary. I hoped that with maturity – growing up – things that were scary now would not be scary later on. I figured the more I learned, the more I would understand things and the more I understood things the less scary life would be. I suddenly missed my books and my mother who had taught me to love them and the wisdom they contained.

Without speaking of it further, we urged our horses up to a slow gallop. I had seldom experienced that back in the city – galloping on the crowded streets was frowned upon – a good way to get in trouble. I liked the way it sent my hair flopping about behind me and how the air in my face provided instant cool for my whole body.

After a few minutes, the horses became skittish – like they did when they spied a snake or smelled a coyote or big cat. They reared up on their hind legs.

"'Smell the air, Macrk!'"

"'Smoke,' " I replied looking all around to find the direction it was coming from.

He pointed to the top of the hill to our right. I could see the smoke rising for a good mile out in front of us. The fire was still down the slope on the other side of the valley.

"'The creek in this valley is too shallow and narrow to be of much help for the animals. The fire will jump it like it wasn't even there. We need to find large rock outcroppings. They may hold a cave.'"

"'Across the creek, there, I said, pointing.'"

He turned and I followed him through the water and across the meadow. He set a fast gallop, which told me things were serious. As we approached the hill, I realized that it was quite steep. The rock formation was well up the side. He dismounted. I dismounted. We led our horses on the trot.

"'There are two good prospects for caves,' " he said. "'You explore the nearest one. I will go on to the second. We must hurry. The fire is moving fast. It has already come down the slope and jumped the stream. Fire spreads up hillside much faster than it burns down one.'"

CHAPTER EIGHT
A Scream Out of the Dark!

Luck was with me. I dismounted and examined what I had – an opening in the rock tall enough for the horses, three yards wide and at least four deep. I returned outside and got Feath's attention, waving my arms over my head. He mounted Pony and came directly to me. The fire had started up the hill on our side of the valley. I could hear it approaching. I had never considered you could hear fire. 'Crackling' or 'snapping' pretty well described it.

"'Great find, Marck. The animals maywill be skittish about entering until the fire is upon us. Then it will happen in a hurry. Wrap the ends of the reins around your wrists to keep a good grip. Can't have our transportation run out on us. They may bolt at the flames.'"

He dismounted and Pony followed him right inside. Black put up a mild fuss but had soon joined us. That part had been simpler than Feath had led me to believe. I hoped the rest went as well.

"'Move toward the back. There may be water for the horses – good water – seepage from inside the hill.'"

There was. How did this boy know that? He knew so many things I didn't. I supposed I knew many things he didn't, also. At the moment it was what he knew that counted. I was happy to followtake his lead and benefit from his knowledge.

"'Keep them facing the rear so the fire and heat don't frighten them. The fire will be moving fast so it will be over as fast as it starts.'"

I figured to keep me facing toward the back was, also, a

good idea. I felt the heat. The cave brightened. The heat left. The cave darkened. Just like Feath had predicted – it was upon us and beyond us almost before it began as the fire rapidly swept on up the hill.

"'We will need to remain in here for few minutes. The limbs and ground will remain hot for short time. The fire moved so fast through the grass, I doubt if most of the trees were permanently damaged. A month from now they will spout new buds and in one month it will look like Spring restarting itself.'"

An hour later, we were back down on the trail. It was largemostly hardpacked dirt so had not been damaged and presented no lingering danger for the horses. Another hour had us well past the area consumed by the fire and things felt back to normal. So many scary things had happened in such a short time, I hadn't had time to be frightened by any of them. I would have to think about that later – was it a good thing or a bad thing?

We rode on in silence, both of us having big decisions to make. We talked things out that evening by the campfire.

"'I think it is time I turn norsouth and find my people,' " Feath said.

"'I understand. I've been expecting that. I have decided to head out west and see if I can get on building the railroad. I can't go home, so I need to get on finding my new life.'"

He nodded. It wasn't a time for smiles – we would miss each other. I was interested in how fast two such different boys could come to care so much about each other. I wondered if those feelings would last once we had gone our separate ways. That didn't matter – what had been, had been good, and I figured that at least some traces of what we had built would remain within each of us.

Having agreed there would be no future between us, wWe had run out of things to talk about, so we turned in early that evening. It was like we were severing our relationship right then and there – putting distance between us. That was best, I figured. No use trying to prolong something that could not continue.

I awoke with the sun in my eyes the next morning. Feath had already left – sometime during the night. I understood I would never see him again. I was aware that I had learned a good deal more from him than he had from me. One thing I hoped he had learned was that there was at least one good, compassionate, honest, and helpful white man in the world – a young Irishman, in fact. Interesting to me – I had also learned that about myself. Good for me!

Perhaps that would become part of my future – to demonstrate to those I met that there were good people in the world – especially, Irishman. It would be a huge undertaking. I hoped I was up to it. That reminded me that I still owed the Home for Black. Once I began earning money, I would save back some part of it each week until I could cover it. I figured fiftyone hundred dollars would be a fair sum.

During the following several weeks, Black and I made our way across what remained of Iowa, following the older railroad tracks, which were in use, of course. I was told they were the ones that hooked up with the new track that began on the far edge of the state. I was in no hurry. Having spent my life shoulder to shoulder with people in the city, it was refreshing, in a way, to experience being on my own, separate from the crowd. I couldn't say it was how I'd want to spend the rest of my life, but it provided a sense of freedom and boosted my self-confidence.

When I encountered a train, I would dismount and wave. The engineer would wave and blow his whistle. Passengers would open the window and also wave. It didn't seem fair that with all the good and friendly people in the world that it only took one to ruin that for all of them.

Nearly two weeks after leaving Feath, I found myself at the western boarder of Iowa. The rail construction was of interest to everyone, and they were eager to direct me to the main construction camp – the base camp they called it. It was where the material and supplies arrived and were later sent on west on by train along the new track as it was laid west.

"'I was told to find Jack,' " I said to a burly, bearded, man who seemed to be supervising operations in the yard.

"'You found him."

"'Name's Mark Henry, Sir. I'm looking for work – work that's meaningful. I figure nothing could be much more meaningful than working on the railroad that is going to tie the east and west sides of our country together. How can I be of help to you?'"

I figured I had stated my position quite clearly.

He looked me over and felt my arms.

"'You're not really built to be part of a railroad construction

crew, son. Give it a few years yet.'"

"'I'm sure you are seeking larger, stronger men, but surely you have some position for a more agile, dependable, hard-working youngster like me. I take orders without question and after a short breaking in period, I'll be up to any task you reasonably require of me.'"

"'You talk like a schoolboy.'"

"'Or a school man considering the situation we are discussing. I am educated through twelfth grade, sirSir, and have read far beyond that on my own. Surely you can't hold that against me.'"

"'It takes big muscles not big brains to carry a man's share of a 400-pound rail.'"

"'I can do accounting – one of the things my mother felt would be a useful skill to fall back on. I can keep track of inventory. I can read anything you might put in front of me and compose whatever documents you might require. My handwriting is quite legible – it has even been referred to as pleasing by some. I suggest you give me one month. If I do not pull my weight by that time, you will owe me nothing but the food I have consumed.'"

"'You make a compelling case for yourself young man.'"

"'Compelling? That also sounds like an educated tongue to me, Sir. It should'll be worth my keep just to have somebody to talk with who uses and understands multisyllabic words.'"

He broke out in laughter, nodding and smiling.

"'I have never held a job interview like this before, Son. I am about to hire an untrained, inexperienced boy – a total stranger – with no references, compelled only because he highly recommends himself.'"

I nodded and smiled.

"'How nice that we understand each other. I have a horse that needs to travel with me and nine dollars and 38 cents in my pocket. I assume you will deduct the costs connected with his transport out of my first month's actual pay.'"

He nodded and had a question.

"'How old are you?'"

"'If there is a lower limit please assume that I meet it.'"

"'I guess you get points for honesty and tenacity – maybe, even creativity. I won't let you hurt yourself, so if I see you can't

handle the work, I'll let you go. You understand?'"

"'Yes, Sir; nothing less than I would expect of you, Mr. . . . I guess I have not been given your last name.'"

"'Just, Jack. It has been good enough for 37 years. It should be enough well into my dotage [old age].'"

"'That's fine with me, Sir – 'Just Jack'. In all honesty, my real name is Mack O'Henry – in case you have a problem hiring an Irishman.'"

He looked me over a second time.

"'An honest, hard-working, Irishman. You know that goes against the long-held picture of the typical Irelander. Stick to your other name or you'll soonget will be, 'Hey Finn' or worse."

"'I have been aware of that since I was a small child. Thank you for understanding.'"

"'My understanding won't be worth the ground you stand on if the others discover your secret. It is in your favor that you speak without a brogue.'"

"'I can, but for reasons you clearly understand, I don't. My father was an immigrant. My mother was born American. I was raised speaking American English. I am fluent in Irish and French if either of those are ever called for.'"

"'Crude and vulgar American is all you will find spoken here.'"

"I can more than handle that – born and raised south side Chicago."

We shared smiles.

With a minimum of direction, I found Black's new home in the cattle car [also called, stock car] and saw to his feed and water. His car was next in line just in front of the tender as the engine as the engine would back the train west. There was a passenger car used by new workers and those who were returning from their week off – one every two months – nonpaid. It was required.

Stock Car

The supply train ran slowly, crossing no more than 200 miles a day. The work head – the end of the new track – at that time was nearly 400 miles beyond the western edge of Iowa, just into the Nebraska Territory – a two-day trip by rail.

I had seen nothing of Johnny with the silver hat band since Feath and I parted. He had not been on the train, so I believed I had lost him. I split my free time between Black's stall and the passenger car – sleeping with Black.

On the evening of the third day, while the train stopped to take on water, I was fashioning a sleep nest for myself in the cattle car; I noticed a rider through the siding slats. He pulled up and spoke with the engineer who pointed ahead to the passenger car. A few minutes later he and a man from the work detail – a supervisor, I would learn – approached the cattle car and loaded his horse into a stall at the other end. I couldn't trust strangers, so I covered myself in straw and waited things out.

In a shroud of steam and the grinding and screeching of slipping wheels, the train began moving west again. We were close to the end of the line.

Although I did not see him close up, I would have known that voice anywhere – Raspy Johnny with the silver hatband with the silver hat band. I understood my job was to stay out of his sight, which meant missing meals in the dining car, provided he stuck around after the train left to make the return trip to Iowa. I had learned the train laid-over as long as several days until the flatbed cars got unloaded.

My plan became obvious; Black and I would leave the train and hide nearby until Johnny made a move – either stayed at the work site or left. He was in control of my immediate future, although he had no way of knowing that. I was in an instant bind; I would be expected to show up for work detail the following morning which would put me out in the open – in plain view for him to see me.

Clearly, he was looking for me. Clearly, he had somehow gotten back on my trail. I had visited the smaller towns along my way west as I searched for the new tracks. I had surely left evidence of my presence here and there – I had not been trying to hide it my presence. That had been foolish. I should have. Where was Feath when I needed him?

"The next morning, I watched with care while Johnny spent the morning casually searching the train. Only once did he approach the workers out front – there were about three dozen of

us, and I found ways of avoiding him. Being a new guy, none of the crew knew me so couldn't identify me when he made inquiries.

On the evening of the fourth day – tonight – I was in the dining car late, hitting up the cook for whatever food he could provide me. He was generous, offering me salt pork and beans, a few hardtack crackers, and a full canteen. From there, I headed for the area between cars, where I could climb to the roof and make my way back to the safety of the cattle car, avoiding Johnny and the men roaming around the ground. The train began moving as it did every evening to close up the gap between it and the new end of the track that had been laid that day.

One thing I hadn't counted on. Apparently, Cook's helper was a snitch for Johnny – paid well, I assumed. No sooner had I mounted the roof than Johnny was up the ladder after me. I knew I had no place to go. I knew I was no match for him in a fight. I was not carrying a gun.

On the roof, I found myself cornered in a place without corners. I turned to face him. He was brandishing a knife – back home called the 'silent killer'. The way he moved with it told me he knew how to use one. I pulled out the knife Feath had carved for me, prepared to do whatever I could to defend myself. He spoke angerly.

"'It's always you and never the Indian kid!'"

"'You make it sound like you like him better than you do me. That really hurts, you know?'"

I realized it was already past time to shut my mouth. Mother was right – I didn't know how. With the food stuffed into my shirt for carrying, I figured I had some protective padding against his knife. I had no idea how to use that to my advantage. I knew about knives – every kid over twelve on the street carried one back in Chicago. I had showed little interest in learning how to use them. The rule my brothers had taught me was, distract with your left hand held high and with your right, sink the knife into the attacker's left side as he faced you. I had almost no time to prepare for his moves. My move worked just like I'd seen it work many times before. I hated having done it. Problem. My knife stuck there in his flesh. Suddenly I was without any weapon. He had cried out in pain and clutched his side but none of that slowed his approach for more than a few seconds. He lowered his knife, ready to lunge at me – the wrong move for him; the right move for me. I kicked at it. I hit it and knocked it from his hand. It bounced once and then off the train. He pulled my knife from his side.

I was feeling some better about things. That didn't last long as he came toward me, backing me to the edge of the roof. I crouched and went for his legs, pulling his ankles forward and upending him flat onto his back. He struggled to stand. He was a tough old bird – I'd give him that. I quickly knelt beside him set to roll him off the train. He raised a knee with great force and caught me under my chin. That pushed me across the roof near the edge and filled my head with bursts of black and white. I struggled to my knees. He was bleeding, badly. Eventually, that would make him lose his strength. Not soon enough.

He grabbed me in a bear hug, and we fell to the top of the car. We rolled to the right. We rolled to the left. He was many times stronger than I was. He was squeezing the breath – the life – out of me. I made a decision. If I remained in his grasp, I would pass out within seconds, and it would all be over for me. My only alternative seemed to be to jump to the ground – from a moving train. I poked my thumbs into his eyes. He screamed and released me putting his hands to his suddenly bloody face. It was less a jump on my part and more a get kicked and shoved off the roof with his feet. I tried to find something to hold onto hoping to ease my fall. There was nothing. I knew I was falling. The next thing I remember is looking up and seeing your face – and feeling the pain in my leg.'

"Wow, Mack. What a story! About enough danger for a lifetime."

"I hope I thanked you, Kim."

"A number of times. It sounds like we need to get your horse off the train as soon as it stops at the forward camp, which I think should have happened by now," Kim said."

"You're right. I guess my head is still a bit scrambled from the fall. Not sure how much help I'll be all banged up like I am."

"We still have a lot of darkness ahead of us tonight. I assume the dirty red cattle car is where the horse is."

It had really been a question.

"That's right. Black is in the front stall."

"Will he come with me without a problem?"

"He's pretty even tempered. I imagine he will. Feath taught

me a trick about that. Here, take my shirt and make sure he gets a good whiff of it right off the bat. He will recognize the scent. That should help. You be careful. The man's nobody to mess with. There is no doubt that I wounded him, but I have no idea how badly. My saddle bags contain guns and ammunition. I have them buried in the oats barrel near Black. Should get them if you can. Don't take any big chances though."

"This seems like the time to go get your things – is it Mark or Mack between us?."

"Let's do Mack. I have no reason to hide it with you."

"Okay, Mack. The train will have stopped up ahead at the forward camp – a quarter of a mile or so from here. Figure it will take me a half hour. I will be back as soon as things allow. We *Yellar Boys* are pretty sneaky and work fast. You still doing okay?"

"Better than I expected. I think we could move on if you get the horse for me to ride."

"We'll see about that when I get back."

"Be careful."

"Always. Another trait of us Yellar Boys."

He flashed a quick smile and disappeared into the darkness.

MackI assessed theour situation. The rails were being laid through a relatively wide, flat, valley between gently sloping hills two hundred yards apart at their bases. The moon was nearly full, but it was wrapped in clouds – thin and wispy, yet thick enough to allow only faint shafts of light to find the ground. That would be both good and bad for Kim. It would provide the protection of darkness, but it would also greatly slow his movement as he evaded the dangers strewn across the ground.

Kim soon saw it would take longer than he expected. The ground was laden with rocks that had been dug and removed from the path of the track. The area was strewn with empty nail kegs and broken and warped wooden ties.

Presently, he was at the stock car. The sliding door was secured with a metal pin through a simple hasp lock. All but three animals had been removed – probably put on a tether so they could graze. He slid the door to his right just far enough so he could slip insideenter. Slender as he was, he only required eight or so inches. He closed it. Some light filtered inside through the openings between the slats that formed the walls. His eyes had adjusted to the darkness.

He heard Black snorting softly at the far end of the car. In the stall next to him was a good sizedsmall donkey. It occurred to Kim that a horse *and* a donkey would be better than just a horse. He figured that since his friend was a citizen and since the car was labeled, *Property of the USA*, it really belonged to him, so it wouldn't be like stealing. Yeah, sure, Kim!

There was another horse at the opposite end – brown – the Johnny man's, he figured from Mack's story. He took the saddle hanging beside it and put it on the donkey – a bit large but that could be fixed. He saddled Black and retrieved the guns from the oats barrel. There was a pull-out ramp that rode under the door opening.

By then, the crew was sleeping or elsewhere. Working quietly, Kim positioned the ramp, led the animals down it to the ground one at a time, slid the ramp back into place, reclosed the door, and had soon delivered the three of them safely into the darkness. The caper took a full hour and Mack had grown concerned.

"Where you been all this time? I figured something terrible had happened to you! What's with the donkey?"'

"My ride. Simple as that. He seems to have adopted me. I couldn't disappoint his little donkey heart! And before you object about dishonesty, remember, that your ride isn't all that legal, either."

"Good point. Think we should move on tonight?"

"Let's see if we can get you onboard Black – see if you are in shape to ride a while."

"Good plan."

Black had gone directly to Macrk and gave him a good nuzzling – clearly glad to be reunited. Donkey took to Kim. It seemed the relationshipspairings had been achieved quite painlessly. Kim tossed his shirt back to Mack and helped him to his feet.

"First, see how it is to just stand there beside Black. I'll get things together and make ready to break camp if you say so."

Mark Mack said, "So!" There was some pleasant chuckling as the boys attempted to get Mark Mack up into the saddle. At last, all seemed well. Donk – the name that easily came to land on the second animal burro – took to the saddle with no problems.

Saddles had clearly been part of his life. They set an easy pace. Mack insisted he was doing fine.

The clouds passed and the world brightened. They could no longer count on the darkness for protection.

"See the gap between the two little peaks there atop the rise to the south?" Kim said. "That's our first objective. I'll tell you the final part of my story as we ride. Just say when you need to stop and rest."

Macrk nodded. The jostling from the ride caused some discomfort for sure, but he would keep that to himself. He knew he needed to get away from Johnny and felt fortunate to have help. He supposed the good thing about having the man on his trail was that Feath was out of danger from him. By then, he could have made it to Canada if he needed to.

Mack wondered how seriously he had injured the man. He felt badly about that part of it but understood it had not been of his choosing. His brother, William, always said he was too softhearted. It was Mark's Mack's opinion that leaving people *alive* was a *good* thing.

They crossed the valley floor and had just begun the climb up the hillside when Black became nervous, stopped, and reared."

"Hey, big fella. What's wrong?"

"A snake, maybe,' Kim said. "Impossible to see in the dark. Let's move off to the left."

They thought it was odd that *both* animals had not reacted to whatever it was. Donk remained quiet and calm.

There came an eerie, high-pitched shriek only a few yards ahead of them.

"A scream?" Mark Mack asked, continuing to try and rein in his ride.

"Like a hurt child screaming out."

"Too loud for a child, I'd say. Maybe a woman."

Kim called out:

"Whose out there? Can we help you? What is wrong?"

It didn't remain a mystery for long. A pair of eyes appeared at knee height not five yards ahead of them. They looked to be on fire. Another scream. Whatever it was, it was moving toward them – slowly, measured, like a cat stalking a mouse.

"A big cat, Macrk. I've heard the men speak of cougars in the area. I figured it was mostly just to scare me. It looks like they succeeded! Cougars are said to scream."

Mark Mack turned to get a gun from his saddle bag. Donk bucked and Kim landed on his back on the ground. There was another scream as the eyes began hurrying toward them through the darkness.

CHAPTER NINE
There Were Clues

Donk headed directly for the animal. It turned on a dime and let fly its rear hooves, pounding it time and time again. The scream turned to cries of pain – terrible pain. Then nothing. The big cat lay silent there in the grass.

MarkMack, still on Black, tossed a six-shooter to Kim who cautiously crept forward to see where the animal lay silenced.

"A cougar for sure, Mack. First one I've seen up close. Smaller than I expected from all the ruckus it put up. Dead as I hoped."

"It seems a shame you know, Kim. It is such a magnificent animal."

"Him or us, Mack."

"Oh, I understand, still . . ."

Kim handed the gun back to his new friend and put his arms around Donk's neck.

"You saved our lives, Donk. Good going! Thanks."

Mack figured Donk had saved itself and the boy's safety was just an added extra. They'd take it regardless of how it came about.

"Being tossed around on Black that way must have been very painful for you," Kim said. "Maybe we need to stop and make camp."

"I'd rather cross the ridge up there so we can have a fire. Warmth seems to help my ankle. The smoke might be seen down at the camp if we made it on this side. I can make it if we go easy."

Kim agreed that all things considered, it was the best plan. He and Donk began leading the way. Climbing a hill always takes longer than it seems it will. Climbing a hill when your life might depend on it seems to taketook forever.

"Will you be able to sleep if we make camp, MarkMack?"

"Not sure. I think we should try. I've spent lots of time the past month with day and night turned around. It's not the best way arrange your life."

They reached the top but in the darkness could tell very little about what lay on the downside.

"The twin peaks are a fine point of reference for folks crossing this hill. I suggest we move far left or right – to avoid other people – before we make camp. We don't need uninvited guests seeing us and passing that on to others."

It had been MarkMack. Kim had the same idea but didn't want to offer it in case Mack was in worsening pain.

"I like that idea. Right or left, then?"

"It seems to be your destination, Kim. I'll leave it up to you. You said you'd share the next part of your story and that seems to be driving the direction."

"Yes, I will and yes it does. Let's go lefleft, then."

They found a good spot some fifty yards to the east – sheltered on two sides and with a good view for miles: south, east, and west. Well, it *would* be a good view once the light of day broke through. They had left north behind them on the back side of the hill with the new rails.

Together, they worked Mark Mack off his horse and onto the ground where he could lean back against the fallen trunk of a once tall oak. First, Kim examined the leg and tightened the binding. It seemed to be good. Mark Mack instructed Kim in how to build a Yellow Feather campfire. The breakaways from the old oak tree above them provided dry, hardwood, kindling. *Thank you Feath!*

Mack moved his leg close to the little fire. It did make it feel better. They combined their food and were soon full – well, full for as long as that ever lasted teen boys.

"I won't be able to sleep," Macrk said.

"Pain?" Kim asked.

"No. More the meeting of the excitement from the past and uncertainty about the future. My head won't stop talking to itself."

"I understand. It is growing chilly. Do I dare put on another log?"

"One should be okay – make it oak. So, instead of sleep, how about the rest of your story?"

Kim hitched himself forward as close to the fire as was comfortable for him, legs folded in front of him. Back in Chicago the boys called that sitting Indian Style. Mack wondered what Indians called it – probably just sitting.

"Okay. I mentioned that I have an envelope of papers that was left for me from the man who appears to be my father. While aboard ship, I had a little time to study them, encouraged by the fact I was actually on my way to America. It was the reason I moved east from California to start my new life in this area in the central part of the country. There is a letter from the man – Jacob Crittenden – that will be the best place to begin, I think. He lays out a puzzle for me to follow – to solve. You will see. Here it is."

He removed it from one of the sacks he carried.

"Dear Boy,

I assume you will be a boy, otherwise nothing I write here will probably be meaningful.

It is with saddened heart I have to leave your mother with child, but things from my past caught up with me and none of us would be safe.

I am a salt - a seaman just in from America - the United States. While there, I won a small gold mine in a card game. I will enclose the deed. It is well hidden off the beaten path away from the other strikes. You will see, I have assigned it to you, attested to by a judge and filed with the government. I want you and your mother to have it. I hope someday you can travel there and claim it.

There have been bad men in my past who may try to take it from you -

they are strong of body but weak of mind. Therefore, I have disguised the mine's location with a series of puzzles I feel certain the child of two smart parents will be able to solve but my dimwitted adversaries will not. Here are those clues.

1 - 1859

2 - Find hare crown along golden boarder

3 - One day south of border {from Wy}

4 - First stand of 1,000 glittering, golden, leaves {aspens}

5 - John Henry resting well {tombstone}

6 - Follow soles {direction feet point}

7 - White face {color of stone facing}

8 - Sideways hole at spring and stream- {cave}

9 - Requires wet, head to toe {whole body wet - underwater}

10 - Arid Fire spikes essential {need dry matches}

11 - Acorns understand {trail of acorns inside leads to the gold}

12 - Heavenly Block fickle tripped {area above shelf is boobytrapped}

13 - Milker hide holders {leather pouches}

14 - *Refrain from trips*
{tripwires and levers in floor that
release blocks from above guarding
access to the gold}
15 - *Use wisely.*

"It just stops right there. No signature. I find that odd."

"Perhaps his way of putting distance between him and the clues. Additional protection for you."

"That makes sense. I had not thought about it that way."

"Doesn't the deed have the location indicated – I thought that was the purpose of a deed – to say exactly where the location of something was. Why not just read that and go find it?"

"There is something odd about the deed. Here, look. First, it has the word AUTHORIZED COPY stamped across the front and it is signed by some local authority. Second, the specific location is blacked out with ink. Third, the Deed Number has been circled and is also written on the back of the document clearly making *it* the important element of this copy of the deed. More of that protection you talked about."

"Hmm. Like you have to find the original to prove the mine is yours. I noticed something else, Kim. Here and here and here: characters of some sort."

"Yes. Chinese characters. This one says my name. This one says the man's name – Jacob Crittenden. This one indicates that he is my father sworn on the Bible – a common method of certifying something is true by seamen.

"It is as if those marks verify the copy as genuine. The same marks will probably be found on the original that has been filed in some government office – in Colorado, I assume. It may be his way of giving a second avenue to obtaining the claim. When you find the mine, you can, of course, just do a new claim in your name – if it is still a secret."

"I could. I hadn't thought of that. Thanks."

They nodded toward each other across the darkness.

"Now, I just have to be as smart as he gave me credit for being back before I was born. Fortunately, I suddenly have *two* smart heads. That should help a lot. Nothing says I am required to figure it all out by myself."

"I'll do what I can, Kim."

"I know you will. Any ideas?"

"I think you should not routinely carry the information with you – just the sheet with the clues on it, I suppose, and we should probably both memorize those fifteen entries. If we do carry it, it should be in several pieces so it can't all fall into the wrong hands. You have any idea if anybody else knows about it?"

"I have one suspicion along that line with no facts to back it up. You will remember that when I first went ashore in San Francisco, a man from the ship followed me and eventually approached me. I complained to a law man, and he forced the man to back off. After that, I kept away from him. I really had no reason to believe he was after my papers. But then, along the trail, that band of riders stopped my stagecoach and asked for me, specifically. No reason was given other than I would be kidnapped for somebody else. I managed to escape them, but you know all that from the first part of my story. The mine is the only thing of value I have."

"Donk brayed as if to say, 'Don't forget me!'"

"How could that man have come upon your secret?"

"He would have had to gain accesses to the papers onboard the ship from the Captain's safe."

"Why wouldn't he have kept the envelope if he found it?"

"He would not have wanted to risk the Captain finding it was missing – that somebody had found a way of getting into his safe. Onboard ships, thieves are punished severely. That's the best I have."

"Here is one other sort of thought," Mack said. "What if that man on your ship was one of the men who was after the deed – like Crittenden suggested – an acquaintance who knew about the mine. Perhaps, he had intentionally gotten hired on as a crew member so he could keep an eye on you and your special possessions? With sailing experience and the Captain down a dozen crewman it seems very possible."

"Interesting. It would mean he had already been closing in on me there in China. Perhaps he was Crittenden's shipmate. As situations suddenly changed with the storm and all, he took advantage of things and, like you suggested, sailed with me to keep me in sight. Wow! That will require serious consideration."

"I suggest we try and get some sleep, now," Marckk said. "We can attend to making a more specific plan in the morning."

"I think the plan is clear," Kim said, "decode the clues and find the gold mine."

Mack nodded. Kim shifted the conversation.

"Before any of that, I need to work some more on that crutch – make it fit you better. It seems just a bit too long. Let me see it."

Not really to their surprise, they were unable to sleep, so decided to move on. Still full from the meal, they loadedloaded the animals and were soon on their way, south. With that one modification, the crutch Kim made was first class. Mack carried it along with the rifle in the scabbard on the saddle.

The moon was full and bright in a clear sky. Still, the world was dark as if it were too big to be adequately lit buy such a small speck in the night sky. Mack had heard the territory referred to as, 'The Big Sky Country'; he believed it.

"So, let's begin thinking about the clues Crittenden left for you. That brings up a point. How do we refer to him – Crittenden or father?"

"Let's stick to the man's name for now."

"Fine!"

"You rode the territory back east of here, MarkMack. Any settlements?"

"Very few settlements. I see what you're getting at – provisions."

"That's right. There is no telling how long following these clues may take us. What do you suggest?"

"The last place I came to was called Cheyenne Town. It's probably most of a day back east and right on the border with Colorado to the south – no more than a few minutes south of the new tracks."

"Agreed then, that we take time for a visit to Cheyenne, first?"

"Okay, Kim, but what do we use for money? We can sell the guns, I suppose."

"I have that pouch of nuggets the stage company gave me. I have used hardly any of them. A bank or assayer can tell us how much we have – maybe exchange it for coins. I'm sure we have enough for supplies."

"Good. Let's make tracks back east for a while. Cheyanne should be almost due east of where we are right now. We can work on the clues while we ride. Our immediate question is, do we find and follow a road, or keep to the back country?"

"Let's just get started cross country and talk about it while we ride. What made you think this was the place to start your search?"

"In the letter, he talked about gold, and the first clue he listed was a date, a year, 1859. I have learned that there have been two major gold rushes out here – the one in 1849 was in California. There was another a decade later in 1859 – it was in Colorado. It is more likely Crittenden would have been out here in 1859 – his apparent age and all."

"I see. Interesting. The *date* led you out here. And let me try more; he said along the new golden boarder, which is why you chose to come here to Colorado to begin the search – Colorado known by the miners as the Golden State.

I think you are going to be good at this, Kim."

"I hope so. One problem. If it turns out to be a good mine, I am going to need to get a larger pouch."

They chuckled, having crossed off clue number one.

"Have you solved any of the others?"

"Just one: *'hare Hare crown along new track route'*. You want to try that one, anyway?"

"Sure. H-a-r-e means rabbit. A crown is something worn on the top of a head. What does a rabbit wear on the top of its head. ? Ah. You already made this easy for me – you have figured it out. A rabbit has ears on top of its head – the twin peaks between which we passed on our way here."

"But in 1859 there was no railroad construction yet," Mack said.

"But there was the gold strike and the nickname given the boarder. And there had long been talk of the rail line. It's building had been interrupted by the war. Then, a coincidence, I guess, when I got here, there were the rabbit ears staring me in the face. Good enough for me."

"Right – that's number two we can check off."

"I assume the rest will be more difficult. He wanted to make sure you got a good start so kept the first few simple."

"What if *Ship Peeker Guy* made a copy of the clues," Mack

asked? He might already be ahead of us."

"I wondered that, too, but if he had the clues, and understood them, why would he have tried to capture me?"

"Good thinking. Too dumb to decode the clues but smart enough to know he needed you. We have to hope you gave him the slip forever at the stagecoach encounter. By the way, that was excellent – what you did there to save the coach and riders."

"And me, don't forget."

"Yes, and yourself."

"So, what is the next clue?"

"Number three: *'One day south of the border'*. I have assumed the 'border' is the one between Colorado and Wyoming – the place of the rabbit ears."

"That makes sense. We'll probably need to go south from the twin peaks – one day's ride – right?"

"Yes, more back and forth travel to and from Cheyenne before we can continue following the clues."

Mack had a confession.

"I know it will be best to be well supplied, like you indicated. I'm very impatient by nature, so often take shortcuts I shouldn't."

"This journey may contain a good lesson for you then, Macrk. My mother used to say, 'There will be many adventures in your life. Take time to enjoy every one of them'."

"A wise mother."

"Yes, she was."

"We Irish tend to be what we call, 'antsy'. It means impulsive and restless. You may need to remind me about that – making sure I enjoy the adventure. I'm glad I'm on this one with you."

"You are not required to come along, you know. I have been meaning to discuss that with you. It reeks of danger."

"You trying to keep this adventure all for yourself?"

Smiles and chuckles. What needed to be said about it had been said.

At the first rays of dawn, Kim stopped and pointed south. The familiar, rolling, green, hills had been left behind in the darkness of the overnight. The growing light of morning gave life to a magnificent new view; tall, sharp-sided, snow-covered mountains the likes of which neither of them had ever imagined. In the still long shadows of the early morning, the snow snuggled in behind the peaks, wore purple hues, which made the snow out in the open appear whiter than either of them had ever seen. The view held a few, long, narrow, soft appearing, waterfalls, emittingreleasing mist steam that rode like lacy wings with the water to valley floors, covering them with layers of the thickest, white, misthaze imaginable. The huge masses of rock varied in color from gray, through browns and tans, to hints of red and even occasional streaks of orange. It was like a rainbow in stone. In places, the clouds hung below the peaks, like the sky had come to visit the land.

They suddenly understood about taking time to appreciate the adventure. They picked up the pace, eager to engagebegin it.

"Tell me about Cheyenne," Kim said.

"It's a small settlement but with the railroad construction just to its north, it has been growing rapidly. Lots of stores and houses are being build. It's about to become incorporated as an official town recognized by the U.S. government."

"Are there girls?"

It was not the question Mack expected, next. He smiled.

"A few. I saw some. They are never allowed to get more than a few yards away from their mothers. It's still more of a man's town than a family town. I suppose that will change when regular train routes are established during the next months."

"Did you talk to any of them?"

"Train routes?"

"No, dunderhead – girls!"

"Closest I came to that was having a few mothers yell at me to put on a shirt. Maybe things will go better for us today."

They rode on in silence, tending to their own thoughts.

Presently, Mack spoke.

"I wish I had more money to put in on the supplies."

"We shouldn't think about things being equal. We'll each contribute what we have to contribute."

Mack nodded. He understood. It was how things had always been back in his neighborhood. The Irish took good care of the Irish to whatever degree they could.

As they drew near, they saw thin strands of smoke rising indicating the presence of chimneys near the horizon. As they looked down upon the settlement from a gentle rise, they determined there were three main east to west streets and quite a few more running north and south connecting them. A water tower stood on the far side of town. A windmill stood close by – probably to power the pump that kept the tower filled, they decided. A water tower out west usually meant a well-organized, forward-looking, community that was there to stay. It probably also meant law and order – a sheriff or marshal. All that should mean a safe place for boys their age.

Before descending the slope into town, they stopped to eat and clean up. Mack's previous experience there suggested if they wanted to get close enough to girls to smell their perfume and exchange smiles, they needed to put on their cleanest looking shirts. They discussed having Mack wear a gun and holster and decided against it. Guns attracted trouble.

About halfway down Main Street – dirt, but wide and rut-free – was a general store. They tied up in front of it. They brushed the trail dust from their clothing. Kim assisted Mack off his horse, handed him his crutch, and removed two, large, empty, canvas bags to carry provisions. They headed toward the door. Two large men who clearly had not taken time to clean up before entering the town, approached them. The one with the beard stepped in to black block their passage and spoke.

"Hey, Yellar Boy. We don't allow Chinks to stay in our town."

"That will work out well, then," Kim said. "I only intend to buy supplies and will be gone within the hour."

"A smart mouth, are you?"

"That was not my intention. I figured the town would appreciate having me spend my money in it."

Mack came to his friend's defense even though he was concerned about having it look like meddling. When nervous or angry, his Irish brogue surfaced. It was easily recognized.

"Like he said, we have no intention of remaining in town, Sir."

"Ah. A Yellar Boy *and* Irish scum."

Mack tried to continue.

"If you will excuse us, we would like to enter the general store – like we said, to purchase supplies. Sooner in, sooner out and on our way."

They tried to move ahead. The big man would not allow that. The other man moved beside him and pushed Kim up against the building.

A small gatheringcrowd was forming. A few of the men called out unpleasant slurs of their own. The boys had each been in situations like that before. It was always scary. That time it was more than that. Mack spoke again – but to the crowd.

"I assume these two don't represent the typical residents of your finde community. Is it your custom to allow these kind to build the reputation of Cheyenne? This sort of incident travels fast and far and will likely be held against all of you."

An older man stepped forward and shook his cane at the men.

"They are not residents of our town, son. I will ask them to leave."

The second man reached out and pushed the old man backward landing him on the ground. Most of the people who had gathered were men and they took steps backward. A woman, holding the hands of a small boy and girl moved forward about to speak. The first man raised his strong arm ready to slap her.

Kim worked his leg in between his and tripped him. He landed on his face in the dirt. There were a few chuckles from the gathering. Enraged, the man got to his feet and moved back toward Kim hurling verbal insults of the most vile nature as he reached out. The mothers covered their children's ears. Taking that as his clue, the second man moved toward Mack who understood what he had to do. It brought back memories. He powereddrove his right fist into the man's belly rendering him unconscious and fighting to breath. Kim grasped the arm coming at him from the first man and, using his hip for leverage, threw him ten feet across the ground. While that man struggled to get to his feet, Kim approached him and applied one quick chop to the back of his neck. He collapsedfell to the ground like a side of beef, unconscious. The men who were gathered there took several more steps away from the boys. Mack pointed to the door, and they entered.

The proprietor approached them, hand out for shakes.

"That was impressive. Jake and Bart – two bad hombres. They won't take the humiliation lightly. Your lives are in danger."

The three of them watched out the large front window. The owner's son arrived from upstairs – maybe ten – clearly with two new heroes. His father spoke.

"Fetch their animals around back to our shed. You boys take whatever you came to get – on the townsfolks – then use the back door and ride like the wind. Hurry now! These two live east of town."

The crowd dispersed. Another man, astride a big, white, horse, arrived and stopped. He dismounted revealing double holsters tied down to his legs. By then, the street had emptied save for the two still on the ground and the new arrival.

The boys had the same thought – a friend of the men had come to town and would most certainly assist them in taking their revenge.

Inappropriately, it seemed, the merchant opened the door and went out onto the wooden sidewalk.

"Sheriff Conrad! Thank goodness. Jake and Bart causing trouble again and – believe it or not – they was bested by a couple a boys. Never seen nothin' like it. A dozen folks saw it and a dozen folks will all bear witness to how it come down."

With the sheriff's arrival, several men moved back across the street to assist him. They dragged the two limp bodies away to the jail. Mack and Kim had just made their exit out back when the big man entered the store through the front.

The proprietor's son reentered the room from the back.

"They're gone, Pop. Weren't they the best ever?"

"Close to it, for sure, son."

"The Chinaman give me a gold nugget to cover what they took."

His father went on to fill in the Sheriff.

* * *

The boys headed west letting the slower, Donk, set the pace.as fast as was comfortable for Donk. They glanced back and forth at each other through long, labored, sighs. Kim spoke first.

"I was afraid your story about the 'plex' was just a teen kid's boast. Seems not! Some move, my friend! Sorry I doubted you."

"And I was afraid that since *your* story didn't include *anything* about a move, that you didn't have one. Boy, was I wrong!"

It was worth nervous chuckles between them – that kind that showed up in your life when you had just narrowly escaped death and still weren't sure that things had really turned out okay!

CHAPTER TEN
An Uninvited Guest!

"The sun's about gone for the day, Kim. Let's make this our stop for the night."

"That looks like a good spot over to our right."

They arranged the animals for the night. Kim was better organized than Mack and took time to sort organize their new, hastily acquired provisions betweenwithin the two sacks – food ready to eat in one and the staples, like flour and sugar, in the other. Mack gathered wood and prepared the fire. It had partly been to be helpful and partly to prove to himself he could handle himself without too much pain.

"You think we're about halfway back to the twin peaks?" Kim asked.

"That's what I was thinking. We were closer to Cheyenne than I thought. If we start with first light we should be back to where we startedthere at the twin peaks before noon. I'm eager to make that turn south and get on with our new adventure."

"I am, too."

"We must continue to be alert, because now we have four bad guys out to get us."

"Four?" Kim asked, puzzled!

"Yours from the ship, mine from my time with Yellow Feather and the two we just left face down in the dirt."

"You think *they* will come after us?"

"From what we heard about them, I don't think it's wise to write them off. We provided them enough humiliation to last their lifetimes."

"I suppose you are right about that."

The night was uneventful, and they were off to an early start the next morning on bellies filled with beans, salt pork, and hardtack [hard trail crackers] a while. They were making good time over gentle terrain. By mid-morning, the day had turned hot.

"Drink up, Kim. There is a good-sized stream in the valley down there where we can fill our canteens and our mounts can drink."

The tall mountains were mostly to the west while what was left of the rolling grassland continued beyond the slope in front of them to the southeast. The slope was gentle – an easy descent for the animals. While Black and Donk enjoyed the water, the boysy talked.

"So, by dusk we should be most of a day south of the twin peaks," Kim said. "That means by then we should be close to the 1,000 glittering trees that are mentioned in the clues. What are they, do you suppose?"

"I bet we'll know them when we come upon them."

"You are saying why waist our time even considering it when we have nothing to go on."

"Is *that* what I'm saying?" Mack said offering a grin in his friend's direction.

"I do tend to worry about things I have no control over. It is a terrible waste of time and adds countless hours of uncertainty and tension to my life. It is a hard habit to break, however."

"Stick candy," Mack offered without clarification.

"Stick candy? I don't understand."

"When something unpleasant or unknown comes up for me, instead of worrying, I imagine a pasture that grows nothing but an endless supply of stick candy – tall, short, thin, fat, red, green – you get the idea. I look them over and think about choosing one. Stops my worrying! Same thing when I can't get to sleep – in that case, sometimes I even wake up the next morning with sticky lips."

"You should have stopped while you were ahead. I'll give it a try – what flavor?"

They had chuckles.

Sundown found them enjoying the aroma of bacon sizzling in their new skillet –, added to their provisions in Cheyenne – and eggs sunny side up – a rare treat. It turned out Kim was a really good cook, therefore, Mack decided to play dumb about such things. Darkness arrived early there in the shadows of the tall mountains to the west. It was a strange sort of darkness – the world was encompassed in it and yet one could still make things out, if faintly – trees, rock formations, patches of brightly colored mountain flowers. They were there and yet they weren't – *strange*. Mack figured it had to do with the huge shadows and reflected light from the snowy mountains but didn't take it further.

"Look at the top of the hill to the east," Mack said pointing slightly behind them.

"The man on horseback? Just a speck at this point."

"Uh huh! Probably don't want him to spot us."

"May be too late. He's starting down the hillside."

"He's a half mile away. I am sure we can see more of him up there in the light than he can see of us down here in the shadows."

It had been Mack. He got to his feet while he continued.

"Let's tether Black and Donk back in the brush. They are larger and sooner seen that us, I'm thinking."

Their fire had been just big enough to cook on and was, buy then, mostly out. What was left of its dark smoke would be hard to see against the blackness of the deep shadow in which they sat. Still, they kept their eyes peeled. Mack removed the rifle and a handgun from his horse, offering the choice to Kim who opted for the six-shooter. They sat again, just beyond the ring of fading light from the fire as it twinkled itself to sleep for the night. It would burn out well before the rider got close.

They watched the man make his way down the hill, directly toward them. Mack was intrigued by how he appeared to be getting larger, the nearer he got.

"We better move back into the bushes, ourselves," Mack said. "Keep the animals quiet, you know."

It had been Kim's understanding as well. They hid the pan in the grass some distance away. Presently, they heard the horse's heavy breathing and it's hooves on the hard ground. Downhill didn't necessarily mean an easy ride for mounts.

It stopped and the man dismounted keeping hold of the

reins at his side. He took time to scan the area with before he moved toward to the fire and kicked at it, mumbling to himself.

"Hmm? A few coals left glowing. Somebody was still here an hour ago. Left in a hurry. Wasn't careful about putting out the fire. Sounds like a kid."

He walked the area looking at the ground – crouching a few times to examine the grass.

He kicked dirt onto the fire to put out the few coals that were still aglow, then mounted up and headed east.

"Whew!" Kim said. "Isn't there a saying in English about something being too close for comfort?"

"There is, my friend, and *that* was it!"

"It is hard to see him anymore – heading east across the darkening hillside," Kim said.

Mack nodded thinking that had to be a good thing.

"I think we should wait a few minutes to make sure he doesn't plan on fooling us by coming back after making a big circle."

"Hadn't thought of that. Glad you are along, *Plex*."

"We make a good team, *Chop*."

Smiles and chuckles into the darkness.

"I was surprised he put out the fire,' Kim said. "It was like he was actually a responsible person."

"Believe me, he only did that to save his own hide from getting caught up in a grass fire. Had nothing to do with benevolence on his part. Not a pleasant experience, you will remember."

Kim nodded.

"Benevolence?"

"Doing the right and helpful thing just because it needs to be done."

Kim nodded again, as if enclosing the question and response in bookends.

"So, do we stay the night here or move on?" Kim asked.

"My vote is to stay here. If he doesn't return within the hour I believe we are safe."

"I was thinking that, too. Spread blankets in here, then?"

"Sounds good. I imagine the air will stay much colder here next to the freezing mountains than we are used to back on the plain."

Kim was impressed with the insight but didn't take it up.

"Which of the four do you think that was, Mack?"

"Well, it was just one, so I think that leaves out our two 'Dirt Faces' from Cheyenne. It leaves your Sailor Guy or my Silver Hatband."

"I didn't see a hatband of any kind, did you?"

"Nope, but it was pretty dark, don't you think?"

"I suppose. We seem to be bBack to where we were last night at this time."

"I suppose, except we now know at least one of them is still after us – or at least is after one of us."

"What about his voice, Mack?"

"He spoke in too much of a whisper for me to get a handle on that. Needed to have him speak louder."

"Not something I want to think about."

"Better to know for sure than have to wonder about it, I'd say," Mack noted."

Kim shrugged, knowing he was right but not wanting to consider it.

To say neither of them slept well would be an under-statement. They awakened to birds singing as they flitted here and there making their wings ready for another day of bird life.

"How about just fruit and hardtack to eat while we get under way this morning," Kim suggested.

"Yes, I'm for that. The sooner we are away from here the safer I will feel."

They had been moving south for a half hour before it became light enough to see fifty yards ahead of them. Every so often they checked behind them. Nothing. They were relieved and pressed on. It seemed the route south was going to be straight, along a wide, valley floor. And *that* was how it was.

As the sun paused directly overhead, Kim pointed up ahead.

"Would you look at that, Mack. Golden leaves. Look!"

And there it was – more like *ten* thousand trees – "Aspens," Mack observed. Their leaves – yellow-white on one side and greenish-yellow on the other – gave the illusion of gold as they twirled in the slightest breeze.

They stopped and dismounted taking in the beautiful scene; the trees ahead for as far as they could see, the tall green grass waving gently in the breeze, and the joyful splashing of the stream that ran the middle of the valley as if wanting to race them to somewhere neither yet knew about.

They took time for long drinks. The stream was ice cold. It was the recently melted run off from the mountain snow. It looked good for a swim, but the very thought caused shivers throughout everything that could shiver. Even Donk didn't remain in it long and he was not one to let anything control what he did. They moved on.

"So, the next clue, Kim?"

"Yes. Here. *'John Henry resting well'.*"

"My first reaction was an old man – John Henry – rocking in a chair on the front porch of his cabin," Kim said. "It is what I have been imagining since first reading it, I mean."

"Interesting. Like we would meet a person who would have some message for you, you think?"

Kim nodded and shrugged. They looked around as they rode.

"The trees cover a lot of territory – a whole lot more now, I'm thinking, than back when Crittenton visited this place years ago. What sort of thing might not change in that amount of time – a place for a message that would just patiently wait for you to arrive someday?"

"Interesting, Mack. Likely not a human, then – they tend to die. Let's go find it."

"I like that kind of optimism, my friend."

As they urged their mounts on, Kim began to spin possibilities.

"Something carved on a tree, something chiseled into a rock, the name of a settlement or store – *'John Henry's' Grocery Store'.*"

"All good possibilities. He added those final two words to the clue for a reason – *resting well.* Spin some ideas about that, Kim."

"I find that hard to do."

"How about 'dead', then," Mack offered. – "Tthat could be considered 'resting well' I imagine. And the amount of time that intervened between then and now wouldn't matter once he was dead.'"

"Interesting. Never had a conversation with a dead person,

however. I wonder how his memory would be!”

Smiles! Shivers!

“Maybe we are looking for a grave or a gravestone that identifies it as *John Henry's*. I suppose it could be in a cemetery or a standalone out in some field.”

“Cemeteries are often alongside churches. Among all these trees, a church steeple would be easereasier to find than a single tombstone.”

“Have I told you how good you are at this, Kim?”

He had, so there was no need to rehash it. Kim spoke, anyway.

“We haven’t seen a person in days – a friendly one on the trail, I mean. Hard to ask for information or directions when there is nobody around.”

“That’s true. You have a suggestion about how to proceed from this point?” Mack asked.

“Since the clues give no indication that we should not continue south, I suggest that we continue south.”

“Makes sense. The trail heading in that direction keeps on ahead of us – at least to the edge of the forest. Beyond that, I guess we’ll see.”

They soon found themselves entering the vast expanse of trees. The world immediately dimmed and cooled. There was a well-defined trail, so they followed it. As had become their style, Mack and Black took the lead. In the semi-darkness, they were surrounded by flickering light as the ever-twisting little leaves caught and tossed the sun’s limited rays this way and that.

“If nothing else, the cool in here provides a nice relief from the mid-day heat,” Kim said. “That stream is tempting.”

It required no response. Mack had set an easy pace. They found themselves in limbo – having no real idea what to look for or how to go about finding out what it was. The single hopeful sign was that the trail continued almost directly south – like required by the clue.

Presently, they came upon a clearing. It set off to their right and was old but not large. Someone was trying to maintain it – keep it from being swallowed up by the forest. They pulled up and surveyed the area. There was a log cabin that had clearly occupied the space for decades. A faint wisp of smoke rose from the chimney at the rear – it was apparently occupied. Behind it was a three-sided shed – upright logs, sharpened to a point and driven into the ground – a good roof. Three yards from the front door was a covered well with a hand-operatworked wooden pump. To the left of the door on the front porch, there sat two wooden chairs and a bench. The window behind the bench was open from the bottom. The window behind the bench was open from the bottom *and* had the barrel of a shotgun resting on the sill pointed in their direction. Occupied, indeed!

Kim saw it first and called Mack's attention to it in low tones.

"Thanks. I see it, now. Let me try something."

Kim had already learned that when Mack said to let him try something, the best course to follow was to duck or hightail it in the other direction. That time he waited.

Mack called out as if he had no idea about the two barrels that were following him.

"Mr. Henry! John Henry! Grampa Henry! It's Mack from Des Moines. Amy Lou's son."

Kim was bewildered and held a shrug for sometime.

Mack was surprised there came a response.

"Ain't no John Henry here. You two be on your way, now."

It was an old man's voice. The curtain moved. They figured they were being studied closely and just may have been failing the test."

"Are you my grampa, Sir?"

"No, now skedaddle. I got you in my sights."

"Why? We're here on a friendly visit. Just two kids. We mean you no harm. Please, talk with us. We've come a long way to find you."

A few moments passed. The gun was removed from its resting place. The door eased open a few inches. Silence. Then:

"Git down and move away from your mounts."

"Thank you, Sir. I'm Mack."

He raised his arms slightly to indicate only good intentions.

"This is my traveling companion, Kim Woo. I have come all the way from Iowa."

The old man opened the door and showed himself, his shotgun at the ready. After looking them over for a few moments, he lowered the barrel but left no doubt it could be raised in seconds if that seemed like the best response.

"John Henry, you say?"

"Yes, Sir. Mother hasn't heard from him for many years. We're on our way south to the gold fields."

"Silliness. Not one in a hundred finds no gold anymore."

"If you're not grampa, do you have a name you're willing to share with us, Sir?"

"Always been called, Boo – jist Boo."

"Can you tell us anything about my Grampa Henry?"

"Dead some years, now."

"I'm sorry. I assume he was your friend."

"Best friends."

"If he is buried nearby, I'd like to pay my respects, Mr. Boo."

"No *Mister* – Just Boo. That's a kindly thing for a youngster to want to do. If you're packin', leave 'em on your horses. An old man alone in the world can't be too careful."

"Oh, we certainly understand that, Boo."

They did as he had requested. They even went further and raised their shirts and turned around slowly.

"Thank ya. Out behind the shed."

As he hitched his head, he motioned with the gun for them to walk ahead of him. Inside a neatly kept, fenced-in plot, there were two markers and space for one more – Boo's, someday – they assumed.

"Move as close as you like. Johnny's on the left. Maybelle, his wife, in the center. Both died of the fever – within a week a each other. I done what I could, but it was the fever, ya know."

There was a black metal gate that matched the fence. They moved inside, knowing exactly what they needed. Kim sketched the layout for future reference.

Mack had one more card up his sleeve.

"May I pick one of those flowers and lay it on his grave, Boo?"

"Guessin' that's okay. They're Mountain Daisies if you don't know. His wife's favorite. It's why I still take care aof them."

That put Mack close enough to read aloud what was on the stone, so Kim could copy it down; His name, dates of birth and death, and the words, 'God Bless his Soul'. It wasn't much to sum up a man's whole life. It wasn't much to provide a clue, either.

"Thank you, Boo. You have been very kind to us. Are you alright? Is there anything you need? Are there things we can do for you while we are here?"

"I'm jist fine, boys. You are nice boys. I'm glad ya stopped by. You tell his sister he was a good man."

"We certainly will take care of that. Thanks again."

It was Mack's Irish heritage that wanted to offer his hand for a shake. Considering the shotgun and all, he decided on a, "Goodbye, Boo. Thanks for the information."

They walked to their mounts and moved on south along the trail. They left a happier old man behind them with fresh memories to ponder.

"I declare, Mack! You concoct lies like a shore makes waves. One after another as if they all just belonged together. For a moment there I was almost believing you, Grandson."

Smiles.

"The skill has saved my hide more than once. Also, got my hide tanned a few times when I was younger. I am more careful about when and where to use it these days."

That was all the explanation he would offer and was more than Kim had requested. They rode on for another twenty minutes where they came upon a smaller clearing. They dismounted and studied the sketch of the burial plot and the words.

"Even if we figured that clue correctly – and it seems that we did – I don't have any idea what it means, do you, Kim?"

"None whatsoever, but, like you, I'm certain we found exactly what the clue intended. Any other interpretation would involve a one in a hundred billion coincidence. We have the name match – John Henry. That has to be the significant feature, right?"

"Right. What is that next clue? Something about – something about his feet?"

"Maybe, I suppose. Says soles – s o l e s as on the bottom of feet not s o u l – spirit. How can we follow the soles of a dead man? I doubt if he's going anywhere."

Smiles with put-on shivers!.

They took long drinks from their canteens and sat in the cool grass. Mack spoke.

"Okay, so his soles are six feet under and aren't going anywhere. How else could we follow them?"

A long silence. The animals enjoyed the short, but apparently satisfyingdelicious grass that matted the forest floor. Kim moved onto his side. Mack lay back with his arms behind his head. Unusual positions seemed to stimulate their thinking.

Somewhat comically, they both offered long sighs at the same moment.

"This is sort of gruesome," Kim began, "but think of John Henry's body layinglying in that grave – head nearest the tombstone, I imagine. Point straight down his legs to the feet and then continue that line beyond the grave – *follow soles* – that imaginary line – to where it points. What do you think?"

"Have I told you that you are really good at this?"

That time they laughed out loud. Mack sat up nodding.

"It's the best we have – and, actually, it's pretty good. Let's give it a try and see if anything reasonable comes of it."

"It's not only the best we have, it's *all* we have the way I see it," Kim said, as he got to his feet and brushed himself free of grass.

Black was ready to move on. Donk was more reluctant to leave that feast of short, moist, green morsels. Donkeys were smart that way – when they could eat they ate and when they could drink, they drank, and when they could rest, they rested. After a few minutes of refiguring the trail they had followed and the position of the grave, they concluded they knew the course to follow. That imaginary line meant they had to leave the trail and move more east than south across the floor of the forest.

"I think we'll be better off leading the animals," Mack said after just a few minutes of batting away low branches. "Make sure we are walking a straight line. Pick a tree some distance up ahead that continues our straight line and head for it. Then another and so on. It will keep us from walking in circles or an irregular line. Learned that from Yellow Feather."

"I could have guessed that, Chicago Boy. I am becoming grateful that he was in your life *before* me."

More smiles. It was true, of course. One of those, *'everybody you ever meet gifts you with something for you to keep forever'*, things.

"Where do you think we are headed," Mack."?"

"You make a good point. We need to have some idea about what we're looking for at the end of the line or we might miss it. What is the next clue? We just whizzed on by that one."

"Let's see, here. 'White face'."

"Oh, my. I'm blank. You?"

"Ninety percent of folks around here have white faces,

Mack. I am still not used to that. Doesn't seem like a very useful clue."

"Remember, we figured they would become more difficult the closer we got to the end of all this. We are assuming it refers to a person's face. What else has a face?"

"Diamonds."

"Got none of those. You?"

"Nope. The moon – the face in the moon?"

"I suppose we could see that from anyplace, though. There'd be no need for this scavenger----- hunt directed by old John Henry."

Silence, as they continued deeper into the forest.

"Right Face or Left Face like in Army drills?" Kim said, knowing it had been a puny possibility before he offered it."

They continued walking for more than an hour.

"Next clearing let's stop. We all need a rest. Must be time to eat, isn't it?"

It was Kim sounding very much like Donk. Actually, he was concerned about Mack's ankle even though he was using the crutch quite well. He continued saying what was on his mind.

"There is an old Chinese proverb. 'By time stomach growls, is past time to eat."

"It is definitely past time to eat, then," Mack said. "Is that really an old Chinese proverb?"

"No. We younger Chinese take the privilege of making up proverbs to meet our needs or desires of the moment. Saying they are old, makes them impossible to check out."

It was the last thing Mack had expected. It tickled his funny bone and called for wet-cheek laughter.

"I guess *we* do that, too. We call them White Lies."

"Seems unreasonable;unreasonable. Who would believe something called a 'white lie'. I can just hear it: 'There's an old American White Lie that says . . .'"

More laughter – tummy jiggling laughter. It effectively broke up the rising tension of the mission and of the uncertainty about the bad guys who had commandeered most every moment of their lives.

They allowed time for jerky and drinks and were on their way again. The area in front of them began to brighten.

"Maybe the other side of the forest is just ahead," Kim said, suddenly appearing less edgy.

He had not admitted it, but the time in the woods had been quite uncomfortable for him. Not only might a bad man jump out from behind any tree, but there was the matter of wolves and coyotes and big cats. He admired his friend for his courage.

Mack had not admitted it, but the time in the woods had been quite uncomfortable for him. Not only might a bad man jump out from behind any tree, but there was the matter of wolves and coyotes and big cats. He admired his friend for his courage.

(Some secrets even best friends don't share!)

As they closed in on the brighter light, they smelled a campfire and all the good things that went with it – food cooking and fresh air rather than the pungent, stale, air from deep within the forest. Black whinnied as horses will do when they unexpectedly come upon others. Donk remained just Donk, completely unimpressed by anything he couldn't eat, drink, or kick.

As they neared the edge, Mack held up his hand and stopped. He was handling himself quite well by that point, in no small thanks to Kim's binding, the crutch, *and* his nagging. They crept as close as they thought they dared, remaining well back inside the cover of the trees and bushes.

What they had figured would be *bright* light was only bright*er* than there inside the forest. It was, actually, late afternoon. There were five men at a campfire, eating and drinking and enjoying life. Their five horses were tethered nearby. The boys weren't close enough to hear the words but many of them must have been very funny.

"At least they are not any of our men," Kim said, clearly relieved.

"That *is* good," Mack added. "It looks like they are prepared to stay the night. A good spot, I'd say – protected by the trees over here and the stone bluff behind them, and water from the little stream that runs off the pond to the south. I just imagine I could live here. I think it is better not to reveal ourselves, what do you think?"

"I agree."

"Let's move back into the trees for the night. Wouldn't want one of them to stumble onto us while they're using the bushes."

As they turned to leave, Mack suddenly turned back and whispered into Kim's ear.

"Wait just a minute, Kim! Did you see what I saw on the other side of the pond?"
"

I did see it! It'll take more light to be sure."
"Yeah. Have to wait for morning. This is exciting!"

CHAPTER ELEVEN
The Eerie Glow at the Back of the Pond

It had been a long day and the journey had taken its toll, so sleep came easily and deep. When they awakened, it was already light. They left the animals tethered and cautiously made their way to the edge of the forest. The men were gone. There was not so much as a bottle or cigar butt left behind. Either they were exceptionally neat men, or they were being extremely cautious.

"My guess is they were wanted men and didn't dare leave any trace behind," Mack said.

"Sounds like our decision to avoid them was a good one," Kim added.

For the first time they were able to look over the area in the light.

"What a nice spot," Kim said. "A pool, a stream, and a nice grassy area. An ideal spot for camping."

Mack agreed and dropped to the grass stretching his legs out in front of him thinking a thorough review of what they knew was in order.

"So, what we saw last night – was that chalky bluff on the other side of their camp site – other side of the large pond the way it looks in the light."

"The chalky – white – *face* of that bluff on the other side," Kim said bringing things back to the clues.

"The white face in the clue, you think?"

"Well, we followed the line that we established back at the little cemetery, and here we are at the base of a white bluff. We sure can't go any further straight ahead. Looks like the end of the trail."

"Right. So, we need to figure out what we need to do with it – the white face in front of us. Probably can't take it with us."

Smiles.

"Time we got back to the clues," Kim said slipping the sheet of paper from his rear pocket and sitting back on his legs beside Mack who was massaging his good leg. The trek through the forest the day before had tired it.

"Here's the next clue: *'Sunken horizontal hole at spring'*. I think it is the strangest of the clues."

"All I get from that is, 'hole at spring'. All I see is spring – the pond right here between us and the bluff – spring fed."

"There are problems in *this* clue for sure," Kim said. "In the first place, I think of holes as being vertical – up and down, not sideways. That would be more like a trench. Second, if something is sunken, how can we see it? Wouldn't sunken mean out of sight?"

"I'd think so. We must take this one as a challenge. We may be overthinking it. What DO we have?"

"Well, we have the white face of the bluff," Kim said taking up Mack's challenge. "Looks to be 25 yards wide and 40 yards high. It's a substantial natural structure. We can see the stream and now we can see it flows out of a small pond that we couldn't see very well in the dark last night."

"We can assume the pond is spring fed, so we have the spring," Mack added. "That leaves *sunken* – in the water, maybe? Things sink in water."

"Maybe. *Likely* even, given the surroundings," Kim said. "I was going to say a horizontal hole could be a cave, but I've looked the bluff up one side and down the other. Don't see anything resembling a cave opening."

They sat back on their legs to examine what lay before them. Mack spoke.

"The cave could be underwater, I suppose. Maybe the next clue will help set us on the right track."

"Okay. Good idea. It says, *'Requires wet, head to toe'*."

"That sounds a whole lot like we're in for more than wading – . Sounds like an underwater swim in our near future," Mack said, putting on a shiver, remembering the cold mountain stream.

"Are you a good swimmer, Kim?"

"Yes, in fact I am very good – stronger than I look. I learned to swim in the ocean just off-shore from my village. More than once I swam my way free of riptides."

"Okay, just collecting information. I'm a good swimmer too. I learned to swim in a huge lake – similar I'd think to swimming near the shore of your ocean. We still seem to be back at a whole lot of nothing. Do you have a suggestion about where to go from here?"

"Let us look the poolit over from up here on its bankabove."

They stood and walked to the edge of the pond, and instinctively leaning down and putting their hands in the water to get a feel for the temperature.

"Cold but not like the mountain stream was," Mack said.

They walked around the edge, taking took some time exploring what they could see through the water – down perhaps six feet into a deep, dark, pool. The shadows of the bluff and the forest met to keep the pool dark. They didn't immediately find any indication of a cave-likesuch an opening in the side. They did find it looked to be a large, deep, bowl made of solid stone.

"Maybe we could use long sticks to probe the sides down below where we can see from up here," Kim suggested.

"Excellent idea. A cave would most likely be in the wall of the pond. Lots of nice straight saplings along the edge of the woods for us to clean up."

They worked on two, straight, little trees for fifteen minutes, stripping them of their branches.at it for fifteen minutes, They wereboth happy with the results – two, pretty good-looking fishing poles. At the rear of the pond was the base of the bluff, which continued downward to form the back side of the pool. The rest was shaped like an irregular oval – a bowl – with thea stream running off to the south – the right as they stood looking at it. The pool was twelve yards end to end and six front to back.

"There is a lot of water coming into the pond – that make's a good amount of water leaving it," Kim noted, pointing to the stream off to their right.

"A powerful spring feeding the pond and in turn, that little creek," Mack added thinking some clarification might be helpful.

Kim agreed with a nod and more silence.

They began probing the sides all aroundbelow the five-foot

level. They figured they would feel the end of their poles slip into any opening – hole – there might be. They poked here and there.

"I suggest we do this more systematically," Kim said. "LetsLet's probe up and down just a couple of feet all the way around. If we don't find anything in the top several feet, we can go around a second time just a bit deeper."

"Excellent. Let's get at it."

They began at opposite ends up against the bluff and worked for some time, eventually meeting about halfway along the outer edge – the front edge. Mack found he was depending less and less on his crutch, which made him more useful in the search.

"Nothing, here."

"Nothing, here."

"Deeper this time!"

"Yup. Deeper."

They returned to where they had each started before and, working the area between two and five feet deep, again madeagain, worked their ways toward each other.

"You realized we're exploring more than eight feet below the surface?"I may have something here," Kim said. "The far-left wall where it turns toward us out from the bluff and about five feet below the surface."

Mack moved to add his stick to the investigation.

"It's an opening for sure. Good work, Kim. From this angle it is impossible to insert sticks this length into it very far."

"If we bound our two sticks together, we could make one probe nearly twenty feet long and could get far enough away to get a better angle – to move the stick inside quite a bit further," Mack said.

"Let's do it."

They worked in silence and the process took less than ten minutes. They used sturdy, young, vines, overlapping the sticks several feet at the center.

"Your arms are longer and stronger, Mack. You manipulate it."

He worked for a few minutes finding the right angle. It had been a good idea and he was soon able to slip it inside some ten feet.

"I'm hitting something at the back of the hole and can't

move it in further."

"The back wall of the cave?" Kim asked. "That's not much of a cave. Can you work the probe back and forth to get a feel for how wide it is inside the opening? The diameter I guess it would be."

Mack moved the stick about.

"Best I can tell, it's like a tunnel that remains about two feet side to side and top to bottom – maybe a little more. Looks like one of us will need to get in and dive down to check it out."

"So far, our find seems quite disappointing, Kim said. Perhaps there is another one that we are yet to find."

"Possible. I really think we need to check this one out in person before we give up on it. It seems to meet the requirements of the clue – horizontal hole, sunk, and one wet Chinaman. We've come too far to dismiss something that might be important. I suggest the person in the water have a rope around his waist and the one up here have hold of the other end. Not knowing what's inside there, we don't want to let anybody get hurt. The one out here can pull the other back to the surface if that's needed."

"We need a signal, like two tugs from the person in the water if he needs assistance."

"That should work." "I was just thinking of it. That's quite a dive. I suppose it's dark down there. That will mean feeling our way."

"If we find an opening like we are looking for, we will first need to see if it is large enough for us to enter."

"Right," Mack agreed. "What do you think of this? One of us stays up here and the other holding one end of a rope that's tied to the other's waist."

"Yes. That's the way to do it."

"You've seen the long reeds growing along the north edge of the pond. I Think reeds are hollow. Maybe we could breath through them so we could stay underwater longer."

Kim smiled at his friend and spoke.

"You know, Mack, I think you just may pretty good at this."

It was worth chuckles. By then, Mack had pulled several of the longest – eight feet or so – and together they explored them: light weight, hollow like they thought, watertight. Mack put one up to his lips and inhaled. It worked – sort of. He reported what he discovered.

"It works but the channel is so small it doesn't provide enough air to keep our lungs full."

"How about bundling two or three together – side by side – so we could pull air from all of them at once – doubling or tripling the amount of air?"

"Excellent! Let me pull some more. Find something to bind them with."

"Vines?"

"That should work – each end and the middle?"

"Sounds good. Let's make up a sample – what – breathing tube, I suppose."

They worked for some time. Each reed was a half-inch or so wide. They were using three making the combined tube nearly an inch wide. It easily fit into a mouth. They each gave it a try right there on dry land. They each approved.

"I think our eagerness to find the cave – which we haven't yet – got before our discovery," Kim said.

They each gave up a sheepish look. They were soon back to exploring the sides of the pond with their long sticks.

"If we don't find the hole at this depth, We'll need to had some length to our probes – we are at about nine feet now."

"Wait, here, Kim. I got something."

He bellied down on the ground and reached his stick until his elbow was just below the surface.

"Pretty sure this is it, Kim. Let's fit our sticks together and see how far into the hole they will go."

The young vines had worked so well with the breathing tube, Kim cut more. It was an easy task – tying the two sicks together.

The hole went directly into the rock base of the bluff. Working across the pond, Mack was able to work the long pole inside the hole or cave or whatever it was.

"Can't get it in further. Seems to blocked by something."

"How far do you think it is from the surface of the water to where the end of the pole stops."

"Well, let's see. How about twenty feet?"

"That's about right, I think."

"So, wWho goes inives it a try first?"

Kim had the suggestionspoke first.

"You are much stronger than I am. Let me go underwater

so you can handle the safety rope out here."

"If you're sure, I think that makes sense."

Ever cautious Kim made another suggestion. I think we need some signals, like one tug from you means pull me up."

"I can't take the breathing tube inside the cave. First, it won't bend and second it isn't long enough. How about, first, I just dive down and examine the cave opening – to what you called the tunnel? I can come up and report what I discover before entering it. That way, I will never be more than a few feet from the surface, and you will also have the same information I have when I finally do enter it."

"Sounds good." You can use the tube for most of that."

It was set. Kim made ready for the swim. He slipped over the side.

"My feet can't touch the bottom even here against the front side. The water's really not that cold. I'm sure my body will adjust rapidly. Toss me the end of the rope."

He tied it in place at his waist and he was down and back relatively quickly.

"Just what we expected – a hole in solid rock, about two feet in diameter. I see nothing to keep me from entering. It is dark inside."

"Okay. Ready to do this, Kim?"

"I am."

Mack stated the obvious."Hand me the tube."

He took several practiced breaths.

"You'll have to keep your mouth around the end of the tube right from the beginning or it will fill up with water."

"I hadn't thought of that. Good. Let's give it a little try – let me practice breathing before I go deep.

They practiced several times. Each time they learned something new. Kim sputtered to the surface.

"Problem. When I blow the air out through the tube it doesn't empty it and I get lots of bad air when I such in for the next ones."

"Solution, Kim. Instead of exhaling through the tube, do that in the water, like blowing bubbles. That done, attach your mouth and suck in your nex"I guess when you can't go in any further, you'll know you are either at the end of the rope or at the back wall of the tunnel."

Kim nodded.

"Let us give it a try, Mack."

"Okay. Let me make sure the rope isn't tangled up here. If something happens up here, I'll just begin reeling you in – okay?"

"I got it. Here I go."

Kim took several deep breaths and sank below the surface. Mack could follow him as he moved down through the water, even though it was quickly dark once he got more than a few feet below the surface. After feeling all around the opening, he entered headfirst and disappeared. After something more than a minute, he returned into the pond and his head broke the surface. He had been underwater for what seemed like a long time. Mack had become concerned.

"It's amazing down there. Plenty of light down as far as the opening. It is big enough so even your big shoulders can easily slip inside. The tunnel is less than two body lengths long. At the back end are a set of crude, natural steps – seven – up to the right. I felt my way and climbed them up into darkness and guess what?"

He didn't wait for a response.

"On the fourth step, my head and shoulders came up out of the water into an open space like a cave filled with air – I could breathe. It was pitch dark. Be thinking about how we could make a series of mirrors to reflect light into the tunnel and up into the cave. I figure the floor of the cave is a good foot above the surface of the water out here. Did I say it's amazing? You have to try it right now. I have no good idea how large the cave is. I hurried out because I was eager to make my report and didn't want to worry you – how long I was staying under. You sure your ankle is up to this?"

"If it isn't, I'll stop."

Kim would take his word on that. They transferred the rope to Mack, and he slipped shoulder-deep into the water. It was cold but, like Kim said, his body adapted to it quickly. His bad ankle didn't pose a problem in the water. He could move easily.

"See you in a few minutes. With air down there, I'll take a

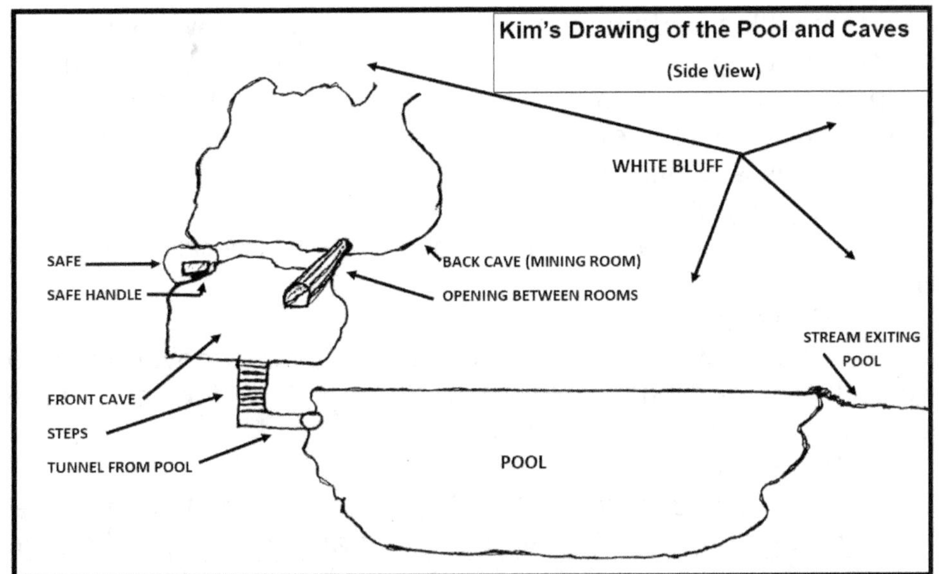

few more minutes than you did so I can feel around and see if I can gage the size – dimensions. He bent into the water and pulled himself toward the opening. Mack was quite strong and moved through the water faster and further with less effort than his friend. He entered the tunnel and disappeared from Kim's view.

Kim waited and waited and waited some more. Suddenly, he saw a mysterious golden glow from the left side of the pond. He wasn't sure how to respond. Like his friend before him, his first inclination was to begin pulling. He had felt no tug, so waited some more.

Presently, down below, Mack figured he had taken too much time so gave the rope a tug and soon surfaced.

"It's even more amazing than you could tell in the dark, Kim. "It is a small cave just above the end of the tunnel like you said – at the top of the steps. It has to be up inside the bluff. It's dry and the air is musty but breathable. There must be a series of cracks in the bluff that feeds it air from the outside – like a chimney effect. It is warmer in there than it has any reason to be, inside solid rock like it appears to be. Warmer, outside, air, I'm thinking."

"What is that light all about? See it?"

Kim pointed out into the pool.

"While I was feeling about the floor up inside the cave, I came upon a large, wide-mouthed, jar beside the entrance. I opened it with some difficulty – the corrosion around the lid. Inside it were candles and matches. Your little cave is now well lit and rapidly growing comfy warm from that single, little, flame. I suppose the glow is from the tunnel opening. There is also a lantern and large can of coal oil [kerosene]."

"That *is* exciting."

"It gets better!"

Clearly, there can be no doubt that somebody has spent time there."

"Crittenden?"

"That's my guess and probably whoever discovered it and worked it before him. I didn't take time to look for gold. None jumped up and bit me, however."

"How large do you think?"

"The main part up front is circular and seems to be ten feet wide and eight feet tall. The back of that area narrows quite a bit into another tunnel. I didn't try to follow it. It could extend another ten feet or a hundred – I have no way of knowing in the dim light. I assume we can easily figure that with time and illumination of some kind."

"That could be a lot of gold?" Kim said.

It was worth a nervous laugh between them.

"What is next?" Kim asked.

"I think 'the next' has to be up *here*. The animals need water I'm sure, and I, for one, am famished."

Kim agreed.

"I never thought I'd say this since my time on the ship, but I have a hankerin' for beans and salt pork," Kim said.

"Sounds fine to me. We just happen to have Cheyanne's best. I'll see if I can dig up some vegetables like Yellow Feather did. I think that kid could survive on grass or thistles if he had to."

Donk snorted. Who knew. He may have been objecting to thistles!

"Throw a saddle on Feath and you and Yellow Feather would have made quite a traveling pair."

It was worth chuckles.

Kim soon had a 'yellow feather fire' underway and the grub heating. Mack returned with some carrots and onions and even a few small potatoes – the real kind that had taken root from the discards of former campers, he figured. He cut them into thin slices, and they were soon also enjoying potatoes fried in finely chopped onions.

"This is the best feast you and I have had in some time," Kim said.

"Probably ever – the two of us," Mack agreed.

The animals enjoyed being in the stream – about knee deep for Donk. The boys tidied up the area like the five men had before them. They agreed it was best to remain invisible in case other people showed up.

"Ready for more exploring?" Mack asked.

"Sure am. This is pretty exciting, so far. Let's look at the next clues. The next one seems simple knowing what we have already discovered. The *'Arid fire sticks,* would be dry matches. How many are left in that jar down there?"

"Several dozen at least. I see you got a big box of matches back in Cheyenne. We need to figure a way to get them down into the cave without getting them wet."

"How about using the jar you found down there? Just keep it tightly sealed coming and going. Maybe seal it with the tallow from a candle."

"Excellent. Once we set up the lantern, we will be in good shape for light – probably light it from the candle I left burning – and won't need to use the candles except in case of emergency."

"I would rather skip the talk about emergencies," Kim said, not really kidding. He continued.

"I think there is a problem while we're down there in the cave, but I already have an idea about solving it," Kim said.

"That's the very best kind of problem – the kind that comes with a solution. Shoot!"

"Time."

"Time? I will need more information, my friend."

"We don't have a clock or timepiece with us. I think it would be good if we had one while we are down there so we can keep track of the time of day."

"Okay. I see the problem. No sun or moon to use. What's your idea, Kim?"

"When we return to the cave, we will estimate how long it has been since you lit that candle – say an hour as an example – and measure how far down the candle has burned – say an inch. There's our time piece – one-inch of burn equals one hour. We can put hourly marks on each candle and figure it that way."

"Yes we can. Ingenious, actually! There's a small wooden crate of candles, so we shouldn't run out for some time. Up here, we will need to put the animals on a long tether so they can graze and drink," Mack said. "There is a nice stand of trees that grows right across the creek a little ways downstream. I discovered it while I was digging things for our feast. The animals will be out of sight there in case anybody comes nosing around."

"Good. I was concerned about what we would do with them. I have been wondering about one other thing – a safety thing like that. If *we* can see the candle's glow in the water during the daylight, it will be even easier to see at night. That would draw unwanted attention if anybody should happen by. This place is out of the way – like the letter said it's well hidden. Still, those men were here last night. At least some folks know of it. We'll need a candle burning for our time piece every time we are inside the cave. Candles make flames and flames make light that clearly reflects itself down the stairs and out the entry tunnel."

"I hadn't considered any of that, Kim. Here's an idea, though. What do you think? My new blanket from Cheyanne is cotton. It will absorb water better than your wool blankets. If we fold it several times long-ways and then make a tight roll of it, one of us could carry it when we dive. If it's wet it will tend to sink with us and not float the way a wool one might. Once inside the cave, we can spread it over the opening. That will surely block the light from entering the pond, don't you think?"

"Solved," Kim said. "This whole thing is better than I could have ever imagined it would be. Aside from being chased by a bunch of men who seem determined to kill us, it's like a vacation. I could have never handled it by myself. Just think how good we've been at it so far. I'm really impressed, and I mean that."

"Me, too. It's amazing how well two 'foreigners' can survive together when they put their minds to it."

Smiles.

They took a moment to study each other's faces. Kim spoke: "That foreigner thing is interesting, isn't it?"

"Things you think are interesting, usually are. Explain."

"An Irishman isn't a foreigner until he leaves Ireland and enters another country. A Chinaman isn't a foreigner until he leaves China and enters another country. Nothing about being a foreigner changes the person in any way other than where he is in relation to where he was. So, if the World was made up of just one huge country, nobody would ever be a foreigner."

"I see. In that case there wouldn't even be such a word, would there? That's fascinating. Thanks for sharing it. You have lots of deep thoughts, you know. Back when *my* family was all living together, mother had a game we played during supper – our evening meal. She'd have us go 'round the table and each say a thought we figured had never been thought before."

"For example . . .?"

"Like, 'how would the world be different if animals had roots and plants could move around on legs'."

"That has lots of interesting possibilities. I'd like for us to play it when things get boring."

"*Boring* hasn't been a problem for us yet has it?"

Chuckles and head shakes.

They went over the campsite one final time, making certain nobody could tell they had been there, took care of the animals, and wet and rolled the blanket. They tied their canvas, supply, bags high in a tree, out of sight. Kim used a length of vine to secure all the jerky they had to his forearm. It was the only ready to eat food that could get wet and not be damaged during the swim to the cave.

"Let's go over the next clues. We can't take the sheet of paper down through the water. Have to leave it with the supplies."

"Okay. Number eleven is *'Acorns understand'*, number twelve is *'Heavenly block fickle tripped'*, number thirteen is *'Milker hide holders'*, and number fourteen, *'Refrain from trips'*. None of them have obvious meanings, Kim said. "We'll have to figure them out as we go. They will probably become meaningful as we consider them with what we find down in the cave."

Kim saw to securing the sheet containing the clues inside one of the supply bags and assured their animals that they would be back soon. Mack stood up without the help of his crutch. He tossed it into the brush, out of sight but accessible whenever needed.

"I have noticed your ankle is doing really good, Mack. Better than I figured, for sure."

"The swelling is almost gone. Suppose it might just be a bad sprain?"

"Might be, but I'd keep treating it like a break until you have had enough time to make sure. That means do not put your full weight on it yet."

Kim was the more cautious of the two and probably the more compassionate. Mack had the edge in smarts and general knowledge. It was a dead heat in the creativity department. They made an excellent pair for their current mission.

Kim had the food and Mack had the blanket and the axe.

They slipped into the water and moved out into the pond to a spot directly above the tunnel opening. It was well lit and easy to find.

"You better go first, Mack. You know the setup inside the cave because you have seen it. I will count to thirty and follow. Okay?"

"Sure. Remember that on this trip, things inside will be lighted for us by the candle."

"That will be a huge help. Should make our entry much faster and less scary – just head for the light."

"Sounds good to me. Here I go."

But before he could *'here I go'* to anywhere, they heard voices – the voices of two men – approaching the pond from inside the forest – apparently on horseback – still two dozen or so yards away.

"You suppose our two bad guys have teamed up on us?" Kim asked.

"*Whatever*, it can't be good," Mack said.

CHAPTER TWELVE
The Bags Were Empty

"*Dive*, Kim! I'll be right behind you!"

He did. A few seconds later, Mack followed. Though close, the men had still not come upon the pond. By then, Mack was quite sure one of the voices was the man with the silver hatband. Kim could not be sure about the other one.

Upon entering the cave, Kim first moved the candle far toward the back, immediately reducing the light upfront near the entrance, hoping it would become too dim to be seen out in the pond. As Mack's head appeared above the water he had already begun unrolling the blanket. He flopped it up onto the floor and out ahead of him. Within seconds they had the opening in the floor covered with a double thickness of the blanket. They felt safer immediately. They sat back catching their breath.

It came to them at the same moment – from inside the cave, they could neither see nor hear the men. That meant they really didn't know if they had found the pond or if their route had led them to just bypass it.

"I think we'll be better off if we act like they came upon our spot," Kim said.

"I agree. That may also mean they will find Black and Donk. I have no doubt that Silver-Headband-Guy will recognize *Black* or at least his saddle – it used to be his. Let's give it all a rest for a few hours. Just before sundown, one of us will need to slip out and see what's going on. They might just move on after deciding we are not in the area."

"And they might not."

Mack explained his thinking on the matter.

"Assume they believe they are closing in on us. They won't want to lose our trail. If there is no sign of us here, don't you suppose they'll move on, not wanting to lose our trail?"

"It makes sense," Kim said. "Sounds like a big part of their decision will depend on whether or not they find our animals."

Mack nodded.

"So, do we just sit here and wait?" Kim asked.

"My vote says let's work the remaining clues and see what we come up with," Mack said. "We haven't considered all the information we have yet."

"I will vote with you on that. We will need to work quietly."

"Next clue, then," Mack said, lowering his voice just a bit. Kim thought it was humorous but didn't mention it.

"I think the clue is, *'Acorns understand'*."

"Acorns cannot understand anything, of course, so what alternatives can we spin?" Kim said.

"First question: What acorns?"

Instinctively, they both looked around feeling somewhat silly about having done it. Acorns didn't grow in a cave. The size of the boy's useful world had suddenly become very small.

"If it had said, 'Small Stones', I'd point out the two rows of tiny stones heading into the rear of this room – the ones on the floor that are half-covered in dust," Mack said. He reached out and picked one up.

They lay six inches apart and formed a twenty-four-inch-wide path from the front of the main room – the first room – into the narrower section leading into the rear room.

"Hey. This isn't a stone. It's an acorn."

Kim reached out and examined another one.

"This one, too."

He got to his knees and began crawling, following the path the two lines formed. It led him deeper into the cave.

"Do I keep following them, Mack? I'll need a candle. It gets dark back here, fast."

"Go for it. I'll light the lantern."

"That reminds me. We need to mark that candle, so we know what time it is."

"Let me figure that while you light the lantern. It's dry so you'll need to fill it," Mack said. "Cut the wick fresh and keep it short – it won't take much of a flame to light the place in here. I'm sure you'll be careful to not spill any. Who knows how long we'll need to light this place."

It was his turn to smile – he sounded just like his mother – *'I'm sure you'll . . .'*

Those things took several minutes. Mack determined that their wild guess of one-inch equals one hour was almost perfect. While he finished marking that candle and several others, a possible problem came to mind.

"Is there still plenty of air for you, Kim? Any dizziness or such. I just want to make sure the flames are not using up the oxygen faster than it is being replenished from outside."

"I don't feel any effects like that. It is a good caution; we will need to stay alert for that."

"I suppose if one of us faints and keels over, we can assume that is happening," Mack said, thinking it would be funnier than it was, once said.

Mack set the candles aside. Kim soon had the lantern working and he continued following the acorn trail.

"After the tunnel – the crawlspace – between the rooms, the cave widens – a lot – back here around the curve – into another room," he indicated back over his shoulder in the loudest whisper he could muster. There are picks and shovels and leather pouches back here. Also, several more lanterns and more cans of coal oil. Hurry! Iron hooks have been driven into cracks near the tops of the walls. There are more across the ceiling. Some are covered in soot. Does that maybe suggest they are hooks to hang lanterns?"

Mack arrived and took note of everything Kim had described.

"I'd say you hit the nail on the head, my friend – how the miner or miners lit the room so they could see to work."

"Look at that wall, Mack – it glitters like snow in the sunshine. The gold, you think?"

"The gold, I know. Millions of good-sized flecks and every so often a solid-colored rock bulge – a nugget. I believe we have come to the end of our search, Kim."

"Do you suppose the acorn trail was anything more than to make sure we found the passage into the back room?"

"No way to tell yet, I suppose. It did that, though. I'm sure we will figure it out."

Mack picked up one of the empty, soft leather pouches, stashed in a wooden crate. Each was about twice the size of his two fists placed side by side.

"No gold in these. What's in those larger wooden crates – be careful?"

"More mining tools – hammers, prybars, chisels – things like that."

Let's stop right here and think through that next clue. It's a real puzzler. What was it, '*Heavenly block fickle tripped'?*"

"That's it, alright. What is a heavenly block do you suppose?"

They thought in silence for some time as they examined the floor and walls of the larger, new area. Mack gave it a try.

"Well, heavenly could mean sky, but not in here."

"Right. Best we can do in here is up or high or ceiling."

The ceiling back there was lower than the one up front. Kim reached up and began a closer examination of the stone dome above them.

"I have to wonder why there are still clues after we have found the source of the gold," Kim asked.

"I wondered that, too. I think we should work through the entire list, don't you? The man had something in mind."

"His list has been good to us so far. I agree."

"It would help if we had any idea what we are looking for – the heavenly reference. No stars in here – no moon."

"How about we go back and start our search from out there? – the first place we would come to?"

"Makes sense."

They crawled back through the smaller opening.

"Maybe no stars but look down here."

"What?"

With his hands, Mack began carefully brushing away the dust on the floor to one side of the path.

"What the?" Kim said.

"Wires. A network of them under the dust off to each side of the acorn path. Pick one and follow it – uncover it as far as it goes. Careful! I'll do the same over here."

They worked with care for some time. Kim spoke first.

"Look here. This wire enters a small hole in the rock beside the entrance to the rear room – it's a foot square and clearly wasn't a natural part of that wall."

"It looks like this one is going to end up at the same rock – probably entering the other end – there – see! Help me uncover it. Careful, now!"

For a couple of teenage boys, there was a whole lot of *careful* going on!

Mack was correct. A second wire crossed under the acorn path through a tube and into the same rock.

"What does the word 'fickle' mean? I'm not familiar with it," Kim asked.

"It has several shades of meaning. It's not a common word for sure. It could mean changeable, volatile, undependable, flighty, unpredictable, or unsteady."

"None of those words is comfortable if they are used to describe this cave. I would prefer words like safe and solid and steady."

Mack smiled.

"I understand. Need to think about this before we chance setting off something, don't you think?"

"Yes."

Mack continued.

"Think about that last word – *tripped*. Those tiny wires can't trip a person. Still, *'trip wire'* is a good term – like part of a warning or protection system. Move or pull on the tripwire and it sets off some sort of reaction that may protect something.

"Nobody here to warn or protect."

"Us!"

"Okay. Yeah. I get it."

"Mack continued thinking out loud. One purpose of a trip wire is to turn something on, or set something off, or at least change something in some way."

"But what?" Kim asked, still as baffled as before the conversation."

"Be careful where we step – avoid the wires. They all seem to be outside of the path. Let's figure out what happens to the wires after they enter the rock."

The 'seeing what' part seemed easy. The wires came out the back and were strung straight up against the wall where they were connected to a metal ring in the ceiling just in front of the passageway between the rooms. Mack thought he had it figured out.

"When the wire is pulled – tripped by somebody stumbling over it – it tugs on this ring. I believe that will release this flat, square, stone that is being held in place by the ring. See?"

"Yes. Makes sense. When the ring is released – pulled out – that flat stone swings out or falls down. Then what, you think?"

"My guess is either lots of smaller stones or a ton of sand is released from a chamber up above and fills the passageway. That would likely harm any people in here. In the least, it will close the passage to the rear. Good luck if you happen to get trapped back there."

"Ingenious! Like you said, a protective system. It protects the actual gold mine. So, what can we do besides be careful?"

Mack pointed to various places across the floor.

"Lots of relatively small, flat pieces of stone chips on the floor in here. Let's stack them up like a column pressing up against that stone with the ring and prop it there so it can't open down. Then things should be safe for us to continue our exploration."

Mack began collecting the stones and Kim began building the prop – larger rocks on the bottom, working his way up with the smaller ones. With the care Kim took, that became a very stable brace.

"Perfect!" Mack said. "I'm going to cut the wires up against the rock they run into – then they should be inactive, don't you think?"

"Sure seems that way. Once cut, they cannot pull out the ring."

He made the cut. Nothing happened. The boys felt relieved.

"Here's an added thing about it all," Mack said. "That path with acorns outlining its outer edges, has no wires in it. I'm thinking it was set in place so we'd follow it to the rear, safe from the wires, so we could get to the place it was safe to work on the wires to the ring – a built in lifesaving device for you – *us* as it turns out."

"That makes sense. Well designed, for sure. Good old Dad!"

Mack noticed the change from 'Crittenden' but kept it to himself.

"Ready for clue number thirteen?" Kim asked.

"Let's hear it."

"*Milker Hide Holders Interred.*"

"Another word I don't know – *interred.*"

"Means buried," Mack said. "Now we just need to figure out *what* is buried, where."

"The 'milker hide holders' are buried, you mean."

"Right."

They grew quiet. A few moments later, Kim spoke.

"This may be way too easy, but say a *milker* is a cow, *hide* means skin and *holders* could mean bags or pouches?"

"So, bags made out of cow hide – leather," Mack said. "Like those we found in the crate in the back room, maybe. But they weren't buried, and they were empty. I'm thinking the ones we are looking for are NOT empty. That *would* be a simple explanation of the phrase, but buried where in a solid rock floor?"

"I think it would be up here in the front room."

What makes you think that, Kim?"

"Okay. Assume the leather bags hold the gold. If an intruder tripped the wire, the back room might become inaccessible – behind the wall of rocks or sand that falls, like you guessed. The rightful owner would need access to the gold he had already mined. SO, he would have hidden it out here in the front room."

"Makes sense, for sure. Buried would usually mean underground."

"But remember, the word was not *buried*, Mack. It was *interred,*" Kim reminded. Does that make a difference?"

"It sure could. Good catch. It might include the meaning, 'hidden' or 'put away for safe keeping'. This floor amounts to an inch of dust on top of a stone slab. Probably not going to dig through rock."

"That pinpoints the area for us to explore – anywhere above the floor here in the front room."

"A good place to begin."

Without voicing a plan between them, they turned their backs to each other and began examining opposite sides of the walls and ceiling.

"There are so many cracks in the rock," Mack said. "Looks like a giant spiderweb. If we are looking for some kind of 'safe' or 'hiding place', I think it should be surrounded by four, straight, precise cracks meeting at the corners – a square or rectangle that can somehow be opened or lowered. Does that make sense?"

"It does. Like a door or drawer. I'm getting excited. Seems we are finally close."

"You've been getting more and more excited for two days – much more and you will explode. What a Chinese mess that would be!"

Smiles but no chuckles. Kim sighed deeply with a studied nod as if resetting himself.

"Isn't there one more clue?" Mack asked.

"Yes. Number fourteen: 'Refrain from trips'. I think we already have accounted for those, haven't we? If I had been leaving the clues, I would have put it earlier in the list."

"I understand."

"Anyway, we have accounted for and deactivated the wires, unless there is another one protecting the 'interred safe' area. Do you see what I mean?"

"Yes, like if we try to open it in the wrong way, some boobytrap may be triggered. This man has proved himself to be a careful person. We could be trapped in here forever. All the gold in the world wouldn't be worth that! We must not get careless and rush things."

They agreed on that without further words. Their search immediately became more cautious. They continued. Kim spoke.

"I have been thinking," Kim said.

"I thought I saw smoke coming out of your ears."

"Ha. Ha. I am serious."

"Sorry. Go ahead."

"What if somebody already beat us to it? What if they come back for more while we're here? What if that is the real reason the men are here? They didn't really follow us, they just knew to come here, and we just kept running on to one another. They aren't after us to lead them to the mine; they just want to put a stop to us."

"Those are scary thoughts."

"You are welcome."

"I never know how to answer, *what if* questions," Mack said. "So far, we haven't seen any evidence of anybody since Crittenden left this place. For example, look at the floor. Before you and I got here and began messing up the dust, it was an inch thick and smooth across the entire floor – level without a mark on it. Wouldn't have been like that if somebody had been in here recently. It has taken years to accumulate this deep and level layer of dust. Even if the gold that had been mined was taken, it sure looks like there's a lot more to be mined in that back room."

"It does not seem like it is really my place, anyway," Kim said. "I have done nothing to earn it, you know."

"It was left to you by somebody who clearly wanted to take care of you – somebody who apparently believed he had the responsibility of taking care of you – a parent. If you don't accept it, it would be like rejecting him."

"I will think about that. Interesting, I must say. You have a way of putting odd twists on things, Mack. Thank you."

They continued with the search. Kim spoke.

"Hey. A set of cracks that form a square. Over here. Could this be it? It is chest high right in front of me. Bring a light closer."

Mack turned around and moved to his side. Kim traced the cracks with his finger to make his find obvious to his friend.

"I think you may have something. These cracks are different from most of them – they are as you said, straight and a bit wider. Looking closer, that slab of rock within the square isn't an exact match to the wall – really close in colors, but see how its design doesn't continue the design in the wall that surrounds it?"

"I see that – same colors – wrong markings. Same for this small rectangular stone right below it – in the center just under the bottom crack."

"Hmm!"

"Hmm!"

"What do you suppose?"

"I suppose we have another problem that we must consider carefully. The bags of gold couldn't be behind this smaller rectangle," Mack said. "It's two inches up and down and six side to side, centered under the larger section we just identified."

"But, at least a few of them could be behind the big square above it," Kim said.

More hmms.

More thoughts.

Mack offered one of his.

"Maybe the smaller one is like a lock or handle or something. We have to manipulate it someway to unlock the bigger one above it."

"That actually makes very good sense. I'd say we have only

two possibilities – pull it out or push it in.”

“See any way to pull it out?” Mack asked, carefully examining the areas with his hands.

They moved in closer and examined it further, eventually deciding that was not the way to go. The crack was so well fitted there wasn’t room for the slenderest of knife blades to slip in and pry it out.

“Push it in, then?” Kim asked still eager but a bit more hesitant.

“Seems to be the only alternative remaining.”

“What if we are wrong?” he asked again.

“There is a third alternative, Kim. Leave it all as it is. I really don’t want to do that, do you?”

“No. So, what next?”

“Assuming the worst for the moment – that it *is* boobytrapped and something we might do causes a ton of sand to fill this room – I think we need to have an escape plan.”

“I like that,” Kim said. “Escape from a solid rock tomb sounds good. Any ideas?”

“One. Before we push that smaller rock, we position ourselves close to the opening in the floor that lets us quickly get ourselves into the water in the pool. If we get in trouble we head into the water and out to the pool.”

“I can live with that,” Kim said. “At least I hope we can. Shall we do it?”

“Sure. I’m game.”

Mack blew out the lantern and moved the candle just far enough away so they could still see the important stones in the wall. It was his hope that would keep light from entering the water in the pool when the blanket got removed.

“I suppose that was all dumb. If the men are out there it won’t matter if there is a light for them to see or not – there will be us to see!”

Kim sat on the edge of the hole ready to pull the blanket aside and quickly shove off through the tunnel. Mack, with the longer arms stood close beside him, ready to enter the water the moment Kim left. It was a good plan, which they both hoped wouldn’t be needed. They really, really, really hoped it wouldn’t be needed! At some point, their hearts had begun beating hard and fast.

"Pressing, now," Mack said.

He placed the tips of his fingers in a row against the smaller stone, hesitated just a moment, and pressed with even pressure across its surface. It moved, receding into the wall several inches under the larger stone. Nothing more happened.

"Nothing – I mean the stone slid into the wall pretty easily but nothing else. It is still sitting there. I suppose that's good because nothing fell on us. But nothing useful happened is what I mean."

Kim turned where he sat so he could look up and study the situation.

"From down here, I can see up inside the underside of the big stone – where the little one left a gap when it moved into the wall. I think there is a part gouged out just inside the top edge of that hole, like a pull handle, on the inside-bottom of the larger one, maybe. If you place your fingers inside, palm up, I will bet you can move that big block by pulling toward your chest."

"I'll give it a try. Still, be ready to leave the moment you hear anything happening."

"I'm ready."

"I'm pulling."

Mack proceeded slowly, with care, hardly breathing.

"Oh, my! When you're right, you're right, Kim. That big rock is only a thin face rock – maybe an inch thick. Here. I can lift it down and set it aside."

It was really heavy, but he managed it – chest, to knee, to floor. That done, he lifted the candle, so it lit the opening in front of his face.

"Get up here and look at this, my friend. The hole behind it is two feet square and extends four feet into the wall – a natural hole the way it looks with an enlarged and squared up front door. It's nearly full of leather pouches – of *full*, leather pouches. There must be four dozen of them. You are rich, my friend!"

Kim jumped to his feet to take a look. He reached in and gently slid a bag to the front of the opening and then out into his hands. He held it close up against his chest.

"It is unbelievably heavy, Mack. You untie the string, so we can see what we have."

The string turned out to be a strand of rawhide – oiled to preserve it, so it took a while to do the untying.

"There. Now, let's pull it apart – open it up."

He lowered it so they could get the first look at the contents at the same time.

"GOLD! Mack."

"GOLD! Kim."

Kim poured a few nuggets into Mack's waiting hands.

"Each one is heavier than any stone the same size I've ever lifted, Mack. That's good, right?"

"Right! Some of the bags are marked with a big 'D'. See! Let's open one of them."

Mack put the nuggets they had removed back inside the big pouch and set it aside on the floor. He reached for one marked with a 'D'. It was even heavier. They soon had it open. Their eyes grew wide. Their hearts pounded even faster.

"Gold Dust," Kim said. "Fine and clean and perfect gold dust. Thousands and thousands of dollars' worth, Mack. Now what?"

"I suggest a bearhug and some jumping up and down remembering how it was when we got excited as little kids!"

They hugged. They jumped. They repeated the celebration several times. Fully unexpected, they each found tears on their cheeks. They were promptly wiped away and not spoken of.

"Well, there is clearly way more than we can carry. I suggest we remove what we believe we can handle and leave the rest for another trip."

"The dust will be worth more per ounce than the nuggets, right?" Kim asked.

"Right. No attached rock to contend with. More good thinking, Kim."

Kim acknowledged that with a quick nod. He had learned to like being called a good thinker. He became serious.

"Before we leave, we need to make sure about the men – are they out there or not?"

"I agree. Suddenly, our danger becomes front and center. That means one of us needs to slip out in the water and take a clandestine look."

"Clandestine?" Kim asked.

"Hidden or private. In our case, 'do it so we are not seen'."

"I figured. Who? When?"

"I say wait until after dark," Mack suggested.

"I'm sure that's best. Look at which one of us is the impatient one now," Kim said referring to himself. "What time does the candle say it is."

"Only about five o'clock. Need to wait until nine, I'd say. If we can sleep we should."

"How will we carry it?" Kim asked.

"When we get the gold outside and on land, let's fashion the blankets we left with our supplies into two-sided bags, twisted in the middle. We can sling one across each animal's back in front of the saddle. That should handle as much as we will want to take along."

The candle had burned low, so he lit a new one – a new clock was in use just that quickly.

They pulled the smaller rock slab back into place in the opening in the wall. Together they lifted the larger one into place. With a few adjustments, it blended in like before and was nearly invisible. They spent time exploring the cave back beyond the second room – the room holding the gold in its walls.

"It just goes on and on, Mack – the wall with the gold flecks."

It didn't seem to call for a response.

"Those pick handles would make pretty good weapons if we come to need them," Mack said.

Kim let it go. Mack clearly knew much more about protecting the two of them than he did. He did, however, take a moment to envision just how he would hold and swing one if it came to that.

They moved two of those handles forward near the escape hole at the very front, hoping the men would be gone and they would not be needed.

"I can see it now, Mack; a head pops up through this hole and it gets clobbered with two axe handles. That image makes me feel safer."

"You may have just invented a new kid's game, 'Whack the Bad Guy in His Head."

"When the way gets clear outside, how do we move these sacks of gold through the water and up onto the grass?" Kim asked. "Gold won't float, you know."

"A good question and 'yes' I do know. Each sack must weigh more than ten pounds. I imagine that's more than one of us could carry while swimming."

"Your idea about using our blankets might help."

"Explain. They are out there, and we are in here."

"Well, we arrange the little bags in the center of the one blanket we do have, and pull the sides and corners up around them, tying the top edges together with our rope. Because of the weight, it may take several trips. Gold is dead weight. Can't count on any buoyancy to help. How much we need to transfer will depend on how much we can carry on the animals. We'll drop the blanket container into the pool from in here. One of us swims the other end of the rope outside and up onto land. Then we pull it through the water and up and out. Once out there, we can do the blanket slings on the animals."

"That should work."

In the light of a single candle set far back into the cave, they managed to get the dozen or so bags they had removed from the wall, onto the center of the blanket – like a pyramid. They secured the top with one end of the rope. It took both of them to lift it, and that was more like bump-dragging it close to the opening.

Presently, nine o'clock candle-time was upon them. Mack would go into the water and find out what was going on at the campsite. They tied the loose end of the rope to his waist – a safety measure so he couldn't lose hold of it. The plan was that once Mack's eyes broke the surface out in the pool, he would tug it once to let Kim know of his safe progress. If he spotted the men he would tug twice. If he were in trouble he would tug it three times and Kim would help pull him back inside. Four tugs meant push the big blanket-bag of gold pouches into the water. As Mack stood in the escape hole, the boys exchanged a lengthy look. They had come a long way together. After a few deep breaths, he submerged and was gone. Kim readied the blanket-bag as close to the edge of the exit hole as he thought he dared.

Mack's plan was to swim underwater to the front edge of the pool – nearest the camp site. The surface of the water in the pool was a good foot below the grassy land that surrounded it. He believed that when he surfaced up against the front rim of that bank, he would remain below the top of that rim and out of sight to anybody up on land. That is what he did.

He broke the surface slowly so there would be no splashing sounds. He gave the rope one tug to signal Kim of his safe progress. He didn't hear voices, although he heard the sounds of horses. Had their animals come loose and gone back to the camp, or might it be they belonged to the men?

He moved to his right toward the narrow end of the pond – as far as he could get from the fire circle. There, he dug his fingers into the side of the earthen bank above the stone basin. He raised himself just high enough to get a quick glimpse of the area.

Flames flickered from the fire. He didn't see a horse so figured it was tethered back among the trees. There was just one man – Mack's man – the man with the silver hatband – the one that should still be suffering from the knife fight. He was sitting close to the fire, whittling. The knife sent shivers up his back. He had seen that before. How could he have followed them? That wasn't important right then. There he was! He would need to be delt with. His weakened physical condition should work to Mack's advantage if they had to go head-to-head again. Where was the other man – Kim's man? There had been two voice, Mack was sure of that.

Carefully, he let himself back down into the water needing time to think. He believed he should get himself back to the cave so they could make plans. As he prepared to submerge for the return trip, there was a deep, angry, voice from above him – it was the unpleasant, raspy voice Mack had come to fear.

CHAPTER THIRTEEN
A Grand Exit!

Startled by the voice, Mack paused just long enough for the man to kneel at the edge, reach down, and grab him by his hair. Mack knew his wet hair would be slippery so figured when he submerged the man's grip would not hold him. Then, all he would have to fear would be random shots into the water!

In those next few seconds, several important and unpredictable events occurred. Kim slipped and fell against the blanket-bag containing the gold and it fell into the water – the entrance tunnel. That having happened, he went ahead and forced it out into the pond – he figured it should remain invisible through the dark water and the passageway needed to be open in case Mack needed to return. Rather than sinking immediately, the air inside the blanket ballooned, and allowed it to rise and bob across the surface just long enough for the man to see it in the light of his campfire. He stood and drew his gun taking pointblank aim at Mack below him in the water. Instinctively, Mack reached up and caught hold of one of his boot heels. That caused the man to lose balance and fall forward into the water. The gun went flying. It became clear, he could not swim, although he did what he could to splash his way toward the sinking blanket-bag hoping for support. Bad idea! His legs got tangled in the rope. The blanket-bag, with all the air finally pushed out of it as the weight of the gold sank it, pulled the man down with it. Kim's head appeared above the surface and Mack called to him.

"Only one man left here. Silver Hat Band guy fell in, got tangled in the rope and just sank with the gold. We need to get on shore so we can try and save him – pull the rope up. Hurry!"

It took longer than they had hoped to get in position up top. They began tugging at the rope. With the two of them pulling, the big blanket-bag moved slowly toward them. By the time it reached the shore, it was up at the surface. The man, however, was not with it. His legs had untangled.

Pulling and pushing, the boys managed the heavily loaded blanket-bag up onto the grassy bank. They forced their gaze down through the water. In the darkness they couldn't see anything. Breathing heavily, they sat back and looked at each other.

"What could have happened to him?" Kim asked.

"My guess is that his lungs filled with water. That extra weight will keep him from floating to the surface. It's possible, I suppose, that he did surface and was washed away over the edge of the pool, downstream. We couldn't have seen that in the darkness."

"I hate that," Kim said.

"Me too. Nobody should have to die that way, not even an evil man like he is – was."

Kim rescued Mack's crutch from the bushes and handed it to him. The campfire behind them felt good. They scooted closer to it. The ruckus had disturbed their animals. The boys moved downstream and found Black and Donk pulling at the tether. The four of them were happy to be safely reunited.

Kim still felt guilty about the man.

"Should we have dived to see if we could find him?"

"The bottom's at least twenty feet deep, Kim. At that depth, the water pressure would have probably broken our eardrums. Besides, by the time we could have got him to the surface six or eight minutes would have passed since he had taken his last breath. People with lungs full of water don't live when they haven't been breathing for that long."

"I suppose what you say is true. Still, I feel really strange about it. I have never been part of a stranger's death."

"I know. Right in the pit of the stomach. I got it, too."

Kim nodded and offered a question:

"Shouldn't we say words over him?"

"I guess."

They stood and put their hands over their hearts. Mack spoke.

"Lord, do what you will with him. We're not in a good position to make unbiased recommendations."

They felt better.

"What happened to the other man, do you think?" Kim asked as they walked with animals back toward the fire.

"Your man? No idea, really. Clearly he's not around here or he'd have put in an appearance by now."

"I suppose the man's horse is ours to take care of," Kim said. "Can't leave it without care. They must have tied their horses back among the trees. I'll go look for them."

"I think we still need to stay together. I'll come with you."

Twenty paces into the search, Mack stopped in his tracks, pointing off to the right.

"A fresh grave," Kim said.

"That probably answers the question about what happened to the man from your ship."

"The one that's been after me, you mean?"

Mack nodded and pointed again, that time to the left – the men's horses.

"It seems suddenly we have some pack animals," Mack said, "all with saddlebags. *That* will make it easier to carry the gold."

And it did. With all the excitement, they were in no position to sleep. By sunrise they were packed, mounted, and ready to head out. They looked back over their shoulders for one final glance. The huge white face of the bluff seemed happy for them.

Kim smiled into Mack's face.

"So, which way, *Hey Finn*?"

"You choose; it's your gold, *Yellar Boy*."

"Oh, no! It's *ours* even up all the way."

"We were headed south, before."

"How about Denver, then. That is south. We can find an assayer and bank down there and begin to get things figured out."

Donk headed out like he had understood the conversation and saw no reason to dawdle. It was worth smiles and chuckles.

The banker was amazed that two boys had been able to mine so much gold. He cautioned them never to show as much as an ounce of it or discuss it in any way. He said they had enough to let them and their someday families live in style for the rest of their lives.

"Oh, my," Kim said. "That doesn't sound at all like me."

"Or me," Mack came back. "We have some big decisions ahead of us."

They did!

* * *

After a few months in Denver, learning about money, making plans, and getting their finances arranged, they went their separate ways, Kim back to San Francisco and Mack to Illinois. Over the next decades Kim established and conducted a successful import business – China to California – eventually having four ships sailing under his name. Working tirelessly, he used much of his riches to make life better for the Chinese Americans who just kept coming in search of a better life. He helped them find it and they, in turn, helped others.

Over time, Mack founded a dozen homes across the mid-west, for troubled boys – homes that helped them find themselves, solve their problems, obtain an education, or learn a trade, and become contributing members of society. (Every boy had a good set of boots, clothing appropriate to the season, and there were no sticks or closets and many, many more happy words each day than harsh ones!) After arranging for his own freedom, he hired the judge that had sentenced him to help him get the many legal things organized. He was eager to help. It turned out he had been terribly frustrated with the unfairness of the legal system he had to work within. They became good friends and worked to change laws to favor the youngsters. Mack's brothers earned their freedom and they and his sisters helped keep the Boy's Homes running smoothly. It became a model method for helping youngsters mend themselves and there were visitors from all over the continent who came to study the revolutionary rehabilitation procedures. [Who would have thought? Help a young man come to see his own potential, learn to like himself, give him a fair shake and wise guidance, and he would become a model citizen – even those incorrigible Irishmen!]

They each married and had wonderful families. Every July first, they each boarded the *Transcontinental Railroad* – one of them riding west and one riding east. Meeting at the twin peaks, they rode south together, through the mountains and flickering trees to their pool. They never failed to leave a Mountain Daisy on John Henry's grave. They sat by the pool, made 'Yellow Feather fires', ate salt pork and beans, recalled old times, and got caught up to date on each other's lives. They also found time to remove a few bags of gold to further support their ever-growing projects.

They lived their lives well. What man could ask for more than that!

The end.

www.ingramcontent.com/pod-product-compliance
Lightning Source LLC
Chambersburg PA
CBHW061532120726
48001CB00004B/1494